finding serendipity

Angelica Banks is not one writer but two. Heather Rose and Danielle Wood have been friends for years, and when they decided to write a book together they chose a pen name, just to make things easy. Heather and Danielle live in Tasmania and have written award-winning novels for adults. They have never written a children's story before, but as they have six children between them (including a set of twins), they have read and enjoyed thousands of children's stories. They had much more fun than you can imagine writing this book, and spent a lot of time eating chocolate custard and strawberries.

Angelica Banks, on behalf of Heather and Danielle, hopes you have as much pleasure *Finding Serendipity* as she did.

www.tuesdaymcgillycuddy.com

finding

serendipity

angelica banks

ALLEN&UNWIN

SYDNEY · MELBOURNE · AUCKLAND · LONDON

Australian Government

This project has been assisted by the Australian Government through the Australia Council, its arts funding and advisory body.

First published in 2013

Copyright © Heather Rose & Danielle Wood writing as Angelica Banks, 2013

All rights reserved. No part of this book may be reproduced or transmitted in any form or by any means, electronic or mechanical, including photocopying, recording or by any information storage and retrieval system, without prior permission in writing from the publisher. The *Australian Copyright Act 1968* (the Act) allows a maximum of one chapter or ten per cent of this book, whichever is the greater, to be photocopied by any educational institution for its educational purposes provided that the educational institution (or body that administers it) has given a remuneration notice to Copyright Agency Limited (CAL) under the *Act*.

Allen & Unwin, 83 Alexander Street, Crows Nest NSW 2065, Australia
Phone: (61 2) 8425 0100, Email: info@allenandunwin.com Web: www. allenandunwin.com

A Cataloguing-in-Publication entry is available from the National Library of Australia – www.trove.nla.gov.au

ISBN: 978 1 74331 031 1

Author Photo: © The Mercury, Hobart
Cover and text design by Design by Committee
Cover and text illustrations by Ali and Josh Durham
Set in 13/17.5 pt Bembo by Toolbox

Teachers' notes available from www.allenandunwin.com

| MIX |
| Paper from responsible sources |
| FSC® C011217 |

The paper in this book is FSC® certified. FSC® promotes environmentally responsible, socially beneficial and economically viable management of the world's forests.

This book was printed in January 2017 by SOS Print + Media Group, 63-65 Burrows Road, Alexandria, NSW 2015, Australia.

20 19 18 17 16 15 14

To BAFFIX,
Every day is magic.

And in memory of
Axel Rooney, best of all dogs.

Chapter One

'GOODBYE, SCHOOL SHOES,' said Tuesday McGillycuddy, dropping her battered black lace-ups into a bin full of lunch wraps and orange peel. It was the end of school, for the day, for the week, for the year. By the time school started again in eight whole weeks, even if those old shoes could be mended, she'd have grown right out of them.

From her bag, Tuesday took her beloved emerald green rollershoes, slipped her feet into them and firmly tied the laces. Then she hoicked her bag onto her back and coasted gleefully out the school gate, her gingery-blonde plaits drifting behind her. Tuesday was reasonably tall for her age, and fast on her rollershoes. She zipped to the end of the street, turned left, carefully crossed a road and glided into the leafy shade of City Park. Waiting for her by the fountain, as usual, was her dog Baxterr, with a double r.

Baxterr was a smallish dog, with a whiskery face and shaggy hair in every conceivable shade of brown. He trotted towards Tuesday, holding his lead in his mouth and waving the hairy curtain of his tail in greeting. Baxterr didn't need a lead, of course, but he didn't mind pretending if it helped keep Tuesday out of trouble with the City Park officials, who were fussy about dog leads and litter and bicycles. Tuesday took Baxterr's lead and together they turned in the direction of home.

'Hang on a minute, doggo, there's something I need to do first,' Tuesday said.

Rummaging in the compartments of her school bag, she found two coins, one gold and one silver. Although the gold one was bigger, and worth more, Tuesday felt certain that it was the silver one she should use. Wishes were silvery things. Maybe because wishes rhymed with fishes.

Tuesday held the silver coin tightly in her hand as if she could somehow squeeze her wish into it. Then she solemnly cast it into the fountain where it plinked into the water. Baxterr put his paws up on the stony rim of the fountain to watch. And all the while Tuesday, with eyes scrunched and fists clenched, wished. *Please, please, oh please.* Finally the coin settled on the smooth tiles at the bottom of the fountain, next to all the other wishes that lay there. Baxterr pricked up his coarse-furred ears and looked at Tuesday quizzically.

Tuesday looked deeply into her dog's golden-brown eyes. In the mirror of his pupils, she could see two tiny images of a girl with slightly messy plaits, blue-green eyes, and eyebrows that had a tendency to scrunch together in puzzlement whenever she was thinking hard, which she often was.

'Come on, Baxterr, you know wishes don't come true if you tell,' Tuesday said. *Please,* she had wished. *Please, please, oh please let today be the day that she finishes the book.*

It was a year since Serendipity Smith's last book, *Vivienne Small and the Mountains of Margolov*, had been published, and on that extraordinary day, queues of excited readers had snaked out of the doors of the bookshops of the world. There were children lined up along streets, around city blocks, down the middle of shopping centres and out into car parks. A year later, almost everyone had read *Vivienne Small and the Mountains of Margolov* and many knew the story by heart. Almost all the copies of *Vivienne Small and the Mountains of Margolov* were tatty and torn with loving, and everyone was desperate to know what would happen to Vivienne Small next.

Tuesday McGillycuddy loved Vivienne Small and her adventures as much as the next person. She couldn't wait to have her very own copy of Serendipity Smith's new book, which was going to be called *Vivienne Small and the Final Battle*. She would snuggle down to read it under her bedcovers by torchlight. As much as anyone else in the world, Tuesday wanted to know where Vivienne would go and what would happen to her when she got there and in what kinds of ingenious ways she would outsmart her arch rival, the monstrous Carsten Mothwood. But that wasn't the only reason—or even the *main* reason—that Tuesday wished Serendipity Smith would finish her book today. The reason that Tuesday hoped Serendipity Smith would finish her book was that, as well as being the most famous writer in the world, Serendipity Smith was Tuesday's mother.

Being such a famous writer meant that Serendipity Smith had a diary that was full of appointments written in pencil, blue pen, black pen and even red pen, all made for her by her assistant, Miss Digby. These appointments were for Serendipity to read in bookshops and appear on talk shows and visit libraries and do radio interviews and make audio recordings of her books. There were appointments for book signings, school visits, meetings with important people, festival launches and art shows. When Serendipity Smith wasn't busy keeping all these appointments, she was busy writing the next Vivienne Small book. But when Serendipity Smith finished *Vivienne Small and the Final Battle*, she would for a short time – at least until she began a new book –

just be Tuesday's mother. Miss Digby would defer all the appointments and Serendipity would close the door to her writing room and take a holiday with Tuesday, and Tuesday's father, and Baxterr, and nothing would disturb them.

Having made her wish, Tuesday took hold of Baxterr's lead and walked to the edge of City Park, then lifted the toes of her rollershoes and let Baxterr tow her all the way home. He galloped along with the wind ruffling his short shaggy coat, his ears pricked, his grin wide, and Tuesday laughing behind him. For a small dog, Baxterr was very strong, and he loved to pull Tuesday along on her rollershoes.

Now because you are very good at spelling, you might have been wondering why Baxterr has two r's on the end of his name, not just one. Well, it's like this. Baxterr with a double r was unfailingly good-natured. He never snapped at small children. He never bounded up to strangers. He had never ever knocked anyone over and he never had to be told, 'Down!' He did not bark if someone was passing by the fence. He did not chew shoes or dribble on school bags. He did not pester Tuesday to play fetch with him every time they went to the park, though he was very fond of catching a frisbee thrown to him on a glorious blue-sky day and could leap higher than you would have imagined possible for a dog of his size. It was true that he did eat rather noisily, and often, but he never made bad smells or noises afterwards.

Baxterr was a thoughtful dog. He considered it his job to collect the mail and the papers when they were posted through the slot in the front door, and he had a way of knowing which letters were for Serendipity and which were for Tuesday's father, Denis. Baxterr deposited Serendipity's mail quietly outside the door of her writing room and left Denis's on the kitchen table. On the rare occasion when Tuesday received a letter–this didn't happen nearly often enough for Tuesday–he would place it on the hall table so Tuesday could see it the moment she arrived home from school.

Baxterr was the best and most civilised of dogs. But if he encountered a person or animal who scared a child, as a large dog had done to Tuesday on her way to school one morning, or a potential thief, such as the strange lady in a blue coat who had been prowling around Tuesday's scooter one afternoon when she had left it outside a shop, then Baxterr would growl in earnest. 'Rrrrrr,' he would say. 'Rrrrrrrrr.' His serious growl was not a noise that was pleasant to hear. It made people get the sort of goosebumps they get if they see a very large spider on the wall beside them.

So that is why Baxterr had a double r at the end of his name. Because although he looked like the kindest, friendliest dog in the world, his growl could be very frightening when he wanted to it be. Baxterr had a heart full of courage, and he felt that his most important job was to protect the people that he loved.

Home, for Tuesday and Baxterr, was a tall brown house on Brown Street. It was the tallest house on the street, and also the narrowest, but this suited Tuesday and her parents. After all, as they would sometimes remind one another, the most important thing about a house was not how big it was, but how many storeys it had.

As usual, Tuesday's father was in the tall brown house on Brown Street, waiting for her to arrive home from school. While his wife was incredibly famous, Denis McGillycuddy was not famous at all, and that was precisely the way he liked it. Denis McGillycuddy had dark, kind eyes and large leaf-shaped ears. The top of his head was perfectly smooth and the remaining hair that grew low on the back of his head and behind his ears was very short and bristly. His eyebrows and moustache were both dark. The moustache was neat and tidy, but his eyebrows were prone to growing wild and Denis often said that one morning he might awake to find birds nesting in them. For reading Denis wore large, round, dark-framed glasses and every day, except on weekends and holidays, he wore a tie. Denis's ties were of every colour and pattern and his habit of dressing every day in a crisp shirt and tie was leftover, he said, from years earlier when he ran a fancy restaurant. But now he ran the tall brown house on Brown Street. He was the oil in the hinges and the battery in the clock. He was the one who made everything run smoothly and the one who made everything tick. He made breakfast, lunch, dinner and phone calls. He put the school notices on the fridge and made all the appointments for dentists, new school shoes and trips to the theatre. He made polka-dot brownies, a tray of which was just coming out of the oven as Tuesday rolled on her heels down the hallway and twirled to a stop at the kitchen table.

'Ah, my seashell, I smell the scent of a summer sojourn,' said Denis with a kiss to the top of Tuesday's head.

Tuesday's father had a way with words. He could make almost any sentence sound exciting and wonderful. Even if it was an observation about homework.

'I must remark upon the mark from Miss Mistlethwaite in mathematics,' he'd once said mildly, peering across the table at Tuesday who was trying not to look embarrassed. 'There's no maths a McGillycuddy cannot master,' Denis had said. 'The trick is sometimes to go slower, not faster.' And Tuesday had smiled, and felt better about her poor results in long division.

Tuesday looked at him with a glint in her eyes.

'A summer sojourn? Dad, are we going to the beach for the holidays? Has she finished it?'

Then Tuesday noticed that Denis had set the kitchen table for three. Or four, if you counted the dish beneath the table that had been set down for Baxterr.

'You think she'll finish today! Don't you, Dad?'

'Completion is conceivable, but cruelly uncertain. But I can report that when I ascended the staircase at lunchtime, the stack of pages on the finished side of the desk was this thick,' he said, holding two of his fingers a long way apart.

Denis cut the hot brownies into large gooey squares. He arranged them on a plate in the middle of the table and slid a turkey-mince cupcake onto the plate beneath the table. Half a heartbeat later, Baxterr had wolfed his treat in a single swallow.

'Go on then,' Denis said to Tuesday, gesturing at the brownies.

'I think I'll wait for Mum,' said Tuesday.

'Good idea,' said Denis.

So Tuesday and her father sat at the table and sipped their tea and played a game of cribbage, a card game that had a little board and matchsticks to count the points. Baxterr lay beneath the table and dozed, although one of his ears was pricked up in the direction of the staircase, waiting for the sound of descending footsteps.

The room in which Serendipity Smith wrote her books was on the top storey of the tall brown house. It had highly polished, honey-coloured floorboards and bookshelves lining all the walls. Books were crammed into the shelves up-ways and sideways, and in no particular order – well, not one that Tuesday could work out. The only other items in Serendipity Smith's writing room were a desk, two chairs (one an upright chair for writing in, and the other a deeply comfortable red velvet chair for reading in), a lamp with red glass beads dripping around the bottom of the shade, and an old-fashioned typewriter which made a reassuring 'ding!' every time Serendipity reached the end of a line.

Tuesday had learned that writing was sometimes a very quiet business. There were long hours when no noise at all came from the inside of her mother's writing room, and Tuesday imagined these were the times when her mother sat very still, curled in her red velvet chair, thinking and imagining her stories into being. And there were other times when Tuesday would hear her mother's typewriter go *click clack click clack click clack ding!*

On those rare and fabulous days when a book was completed, Serendipity would race down the stairs and come skipping into the kitchen. She'd kiss Tuesday's father smack on the lips and catch Tuesday up in her arms and whirl her around and say, 'Wheeeee! I've finiiiissshhheed!' That night, over dinner, instead of saying *hmmm?* when Denis or Tuesday said *please pass the sauce*, she would sing a song, all about sauce, of course, delivered by a horse, with unnecessary force, on a long racecourse. Or she would play the spoons on the tabletop, rattling out a tinny melody, with Tuesday on the glassware and Denis on the salt and pepper grinders, the three of them making clicking noises with their tongues in their cheeks, just like a normal family.

And that was just the beginning. Because then there was the holiday. Not a very long holiday, mind, because when readers all over the world are waiting for your stories to be written, you can't let them down. But the weeks after Serendipity finished a book and took a holiday with Tuesday and Denis and Baxterr were the most wonderful weeks Tuesday could remember in her whole life.

Sitting at the kitchen table, Tuesday wondered what her mother and father had planned for this holiday. *A summer sojourn*, her dad had said. Perhaps that meant the beach, but it might equally mean walking in the mountains, or sailing on a yacht, which Tuesday had never tried, although she dearly wanted to. Or it might mean a tropical island with palm trees and a long white sandy beach and a little house with a thatched roof. Tuesday took a deep and hopeful breath, her father looked up and smiled, and Baxterr gave a little *ruff* as if he approved of all this daydreaming. But still no sound came from upstairs, and the brownies grew cool on the plate.

After they had played two games of cribbage, plus a game of snap, Tuesday fetched her book and settled into the window seat in the kitchen. Denis brought her a brownie on a plate and then sat at the kitchen table with his crossword, asking Tuesday for help as he went along. While they deliberated over 11 down and 23 across, Baxterr snored. Outside the kitchen window the day turned from afternoon to twilight. The hands on the kitchen clock made one slow, slow circle and then another. At seven o'clock, Denis made his special cheese-on-ham-on-more-cheese toast with tomato relish and, though it was one of Tuesday's favourite meals, she didn't enjoy it as much as usual. All the waiting had made the fizzing excitement inside of her go flat, just as if she were a glass of lemonade left for too long on the bench. As Tuesday washed up and Denis dried and put the plates and cups away, he looked at his daughter with fond concern.

'How about a couplet or two?' he said, tweaking one of Tuesday's plaits lightly. 'Hmm?'

His eyes twinkled as he said in a wonderfully theatrical voice:

'The butter from Dorothy's crumpet,
Dripped into the bell of her trumpet.'

Ordinarily, this would have Tuesday replying with a couplet of her own.

'Sweet young Edgar, eating jello,
Dropped a spoonful onto his cello.'

But tonight her heart just wasn't in it.

'It's no good, Dad,' she said. 'I can't think about anything but Mum. Do you think she's ever coming down?'

'It is getting late,' her father agreed. 'Why don't you tootle on upstairs and have a listen outside her door.'

So Tuesday kicked off her rollershoes and tiptoed quietly up the stairs to the landing outside her mother's writing room, and Baxterr followed. Tuesday put her ear against the solid timber of the door. And Baxterr did the same.

There they stood, for quite some time, until they were certain that what they could hear inside was … absolutely nothing.

Then Tuesday did hear a sound. It was a creaking kind of sound. Nothing like the *click clack click clack ding* of her mother's typewriter.

She listened harder. *Creak, creak.* Perhaps her mother was pacing the floor. Perhaps she was trying to figure out the very, very last sentence of *Vivienne Small and the Final Battle.* Tuesday wondered if she should go in. Perhaps she could help? It couldn't be much harder than figuring out the answer to 23 across. Suddenly the creaking got louder, and Tuesday realised it was the sound of her father climbing the stairs behind her.

'Well?' Denis asked.

'Nothing. I can't hear a thing,' Tuesday told him dejectedly.

'Odd,' her father said, looking up through a skylight in the ceiling into an evening sky spotted with stars.

Denis put his own ear to the door. Hearing nothing, he knocked lightly.

'Serendipity?' he called.

There was no answer.

'Serendipity?' This time he called a little louder.

'Mum?' called Tuesday.

'Woof?' barked Baxterr.

Nothing. No reply. No sound at all.

17

'I think,' Denis said to Tuesday, 'that there is only one thing for it.'

He turned the handle of the door, and carefully pushed it open. In the room with the honey-coloured floorboards and shelves in which all the books were piled higgledy-piggledy, was … a desk, two chairs, a lamp, a typewriter and a window that stretched almost to the ceiling. The window was wide open and Serendipity Smith was nowhere to be seen.

Chapter Two

Tuesday was confused. Had her mother somehow left the house without them realising it? Was she in the bathroom, perhaps? Or in her bedroom? Tuesday looked at her father, who did not–she thought–seem as surprised as he ought to. Denis stood for a moment, thinking.

'Dad, where's Mum?' Tuesday asked, cold shivers running down her legs and up into her hair.

Denis walked across the room, flung his head out the writing room window and peered into the darkness beyond. Tuesday wondered what on earth he was thinking. That her mother had flown away?

'Dad,' Tuesday said, 'is Mum okay? She didn't fall?'

'Oh, good gracious no, Tuesday,' said Denis, pulling her close against him and continuing to look far out into the night sky.

'Well?' she asked. 'Where is she?'

'Hmmmmm,' he said, non-committally, gazing intently at a distant star.

'Dad? You know, don't you? You know where she's gone.'

'Yes, sweetheart, I think I do,' said Denis, pulling himself back in from the window.

'Well?'

An uncertain look passed over his face. He tapped the large stack of white pages beside the typewriter with his fingertips.

'I can't tell you,' he said gently.

'But ...' said Tuesday.

'I'm sorry, Tuesday, I can't tell you, but I am sure she'll be back very soon.'

'Back? But where's she gone?'

'Well, let's just say she's gone somewhere very important, and I think we'd best leave her to it.'

'But aren't you going to shut the window?'

Tuesday asked, looking back as her father ushered her out of the room.

'Oh, no, we'll leave it open, I think,' said Denis, as he closed the door behind them.

This was too much for Tuesday.

'But ... why? I mean, why is the window wide open anyway? How do you know someone hasn't kidnapped her? How do you know she didn't fall out the window and is right now caught in the top of the tree outside waiting for us to come and rescue her?'

Her father chuckled.

'I know that it's immensely irritating that I cannot illuminate the issue, my impetuous imp, but your mother's return, I assure you, is imminent, though probably not immediate. What *is* immediate at this moment, however, is your bedtime.'

'But ...' said Tuesday.

'Butterfly,' said Denis.

'Buttonhole,' said Tuesday, unable to stop herself.

'Buttinski,' said Denis.

'Oh, so rude! Buttock,' said Tuesday.

'Butter dish!' said Denis.

21

'Button mushroom!' said Tuesday, and before she knew it she was in bed in her cupcake pyjamas with her teeth cleaned, and her dad kissing her goodnight.

'Are you *sure* Mum's all right?' Tuesday asked, looking into his brown eyes. 'Can't you tell me where she is?'

'She'll be back for breakfast,' Denis said. 'And we'll have blueberry pancakes.'

As he left the room, Denis did not switch off the bedside light, nor did he close the door, which was just the way Tuesday liked it.

Curled up in her bed, with Baxterr snoring in his basket beside her, Tuesday watched the light from the moon make watery patterns on her ceiling and wondered where her mother was, and why her father had seemed to be looking for her out of the window, a window that was five storeys above the street. It was a mystery and she couldn't solve it, no matter how hard she tried.

She rolled over and turned on her iPod. Her favourite audio book was *I Know about Vivienne*

Small read by her very own mother, the author Serendipity Smith. It was the first of the Vivienne Small stories and Serendipity had written it just after Tuesday was born. At the start was the dedication: *To TM, every day is magic.* In fact at the beginning of every Vivienne Small book there was a dedication to TM – each time with a different message.

No one in the whole world, other than Serendipity, Tuesday, Denis, Baxterr, and of course Serendipity's assistant, Miss Digby, knew who TM was, because when Serendipity Smith did her book talks and signings and television shows and bookshop appearances, she would never tell. And that wasn't the only secret Serendipity Smith, the most famous writer in all the world, kept from the journalists and interviewers who wanted to know everything about her life.

Journalists and interviewers all believed that Serendipity Smith lived on the top floor of the most famous hotel in the city; she had no children and no husband and certainly no dog. The Serendipity Smith everyone saw at bookstores and on television was very tall with wild red hair.

She wore velvet coats in every colour, long purple boots and fabulous glasses. It was rumoured that she wrote day and night, which was why she was so rarely seen in public. Room service trays piled up in the hallway outside her room, barely touched, and the hotel's maids removed rubbish bins overflowing with pencil shavings.

When Serendipity Smith strode through the hotel foyer of the most famous hotel in the city, people gasped and pointed, cameras flashed and fans raced up asking her to sign copies of her books. But a little while later, when an ordinary-looking woman with a short brown bob, wearing jeans, black boots and a short black coat, emerged from the hotel and hailed a cab to take her to Brown Street, no one paid any attention. When Tuesday's mother arrived at school to do canteen duty, or to help with the school fair, no one called her Serendipity. They called her Sarah, or Mrs McGillycuddy. When children at school talked about the Vivienne Small books, Tuesday never said, 'My mum wrote them,' even though she sometimes felt she would burst with the effort of keeping it a secret.

For years Tuesday herself had no idea that her

mother was anything other than, well, her mother, the writer who worked in her writing room at the top of the house. But when they thought she was old enough, Denis and Serendipity had given Tuesday her very first Vivienne Small book and told her the truth. They had told Tuesday how vitally important it was that she never whispered a word to anyone of her mother's secret identity. And Tuesday never had.

Because just as it never occurred to anybody that Tuesday's mum was more than she seemed, it never occurred to anybody that Serendipity Smith, the most famous author in all the world, was actually in disguise. And that's why it was possible for Tuesday and her mother and her father to take holidays together and never be recognised. They could play frisbee in the park on Saturdays and have brunch at the local cafe on Sundays without anyone ever troubling them. So Tuesday always found a way to keep the secret and the mystery of all those books dedicated to TM remained unsolved.

25

Tuesday lay in bed and listened to the recording of *I Know about Vivienne Small*. Her mother's voice sounded far away, not close and cosy as it usually did. A little while later, after quite a bit of thinking and quite a bit of frowning, Tuesday fell into one of those strange sleeps where you're sure you're still awake. When Tuesday did wake up from this peculiar half-sleep, it was very late at night and the house was absolutely still. Surely her mother had come home by now?

Very quietly, Tuesday crept out of bed past Baxterr and made her way down the stairs to her parents' bedroom. From the doorway she could make out only one sleeping form—her father's. Tuesday tiptoed back to her room, glancing up the stairs as she went, but there was no light coming from under the door of her mother's writing room, and no *click clack click clack* of the typewriter as her mother wrote late into the night, as she sometimes did. There were no lights on downstairs in the kitchen, or in any of the other rooms in the house. Her mother was still not home.

Despondently Tuesday slipped back into bed.

Pressing PLAY, she hoped the story would lull her back to sleep.

Mothwood took yet another length of twine ... her mother's voice read ... *and knotted it tightly about the neck of the foul-smelling sack containing Vivienne Small and two impossibly heavy ingots of lead. Within, Vivienne bided her time. Satisfied with his handiwork, Mothwood dragged the sack along the ship's deck, towards a gap in the railing. The ingots bumped bruisingly against Vivienne's arms and legs. 'What a glorious day,' said Mothwood in his rasping voice. 'The day that Vivienne Small meets her utterly inglorious end, drowned like a cat in a squall.' And then, using all his strength, he hauled the sack over the side of* The Silverfish. *Down, down, down went the sack and cold, cold, cold was the salt water that swamped Vivienne, rushing in over her mouth and nose and chilling her through as the sack plummeted into the ocean's depths.*

Tuesday pressed STOP, her heart beating fast, as it did every time she reached this part of the story.

Tonight, with her mother missing, it seemed more frightening than ever, even though she knew perfectly well that Vivienne would escape by slipping her knife from where she had hidden it inside her boot, while holding her breath in the way she had learned from the sea-people of Xunchilla. Vivienne was always prepared and she knew useful things. She always found her way out of a fix.

Tuesday looked up at her ceiling and wondered what Vivienne would do if she were in her place. Tuesday knew that there was no way Vivienne Small would just lie there, listening to stories, while someone might be in terrible peril. Vivienne would scale mountains, ford snowdrifts, swim oceans. Vivienne would leap over yawning abysses with her small, blue wings outspread. She would battle carnivorous creatures, outsmart toothless oracles, render senseless the deadliest enemies with darts from her Lucretian blowpipe. But Vivienne would never, ever, just go to bed and wait to see what happened in the morning. Vivienne would work out what needed to be done and do it.

Tuesday swung herself out of bed, and this time

as soon as her feet touched the floor, Baxterr's eyes flew open. He got to his feet, shook himself and looked at Tuesday with pricked ears.

'Come on, doggo,' she said. 'I don't know how, but we're going to find Mum.'

Tuesday and Baxterr quietly took the stairs to the top floor of the house. Tuesday opened her mother's office door. Moonlight flooded across the floor. The deep red reading chair looked enormous in the darkness. So did her mother's desk. And so did the window that was opened wide to the night sky.

Tuesday switched on the lamp with the fringe of red beads, making the room glow with a soft, ruby light. For the first time ever, Tuesday sat alone on the chair at her mother's writing desk. On the right-hand side of the desk was a big, thick stack of pages. It was, Tuesday knew, the manuscript of *Vivienne Small and the Final Battle*. Serendipity had stacked the pages upside down, so that the page on the very top was the last page that she had written.

Tuesday was tempted. She reached out and lifted one corner of that very top page ... and stopped. Reading the end of a book before you've read the beginning, Tuesday knew, was a sure way to spoil it. And she also felt that it would be wrong to read any pages of the book before her mother had said it was ready. She let the corner of the page fall back into place, put her hands on the edge of the desk, and stared out the open window into the night sky above the city.

'Mum?' she whispered.

And then Tuesday noticed that sitting in front of her mother's typewriter was a tiny silver box. Tuesday had never seen this box before. It was smooth and shiny, without any markings or engravings. Tuesday lifted the lid. Inside the box was a silver thread. Very gently she reached out and touched it. It moved a little and then lifted up and floated in the air. Tuesday had never seen anything like it. It wasn't a thread from a dress or a scarf. It wasn't even a thread of moonlight, though it was soft and shimmery the way moonlight is. Once she had guided the thread very gently onto her fingertip, she could see it wasn't a thread at all. It was two silver words joined by something invisible. And those words were ... *The End*.

30

The End! Were these the last two words her mother had written? Tuesday wondered. The very last words of her mother's new book? But why were they here, in a box? Why weren't they on the page?

'I have an idea,' Tuesday said to Baxterr.

She picked up the last page her mother had written and turned it over. It only had a few sentences at the very top. She deliberately didn't read them, looking instead at the big blank space on the rest of the page. Very carefully she lifted the silvery words and placed them on the page. They shimmered for a moment before they dissolved into thin air.

'Oh, no,' said Tuesday guiltily.

'Ruff,' said Baxterr, who was transfixed by the open window.

'You're no help at all,' she said to him.

Tuesday picked up the little silver box to close the lid and saw that the words were somehow back inside. She tried again, lifting *The End* from the box onto the last page of her mother's manuscript, but once again it disappeared and returned to the box as if by magic.

Next, Tuesday took from the top drawer of her mother's desk a new sheet of blank paper. She threaded it into the typewriter just as she had seen her mother do, curling the paper around the big, smooth, black cylinder that looked like a rolling pin and placing the hinged silver bar on the paper to keep it snug while she typed.

Tuesday had longed for this moment, but she had never dared to ask her mother if she might write something—just a page, or perhaps just a paragraph, or only a sentence—on this lovely old typewriter. She sat up very straight in the chair and then, taking a deep breath, she reached out and pressed her fingers down onto the keys. *The End*, she wrote.

Tuesday had thought that maybe something would happen if she typed those two words on the page. But nothing happened. *The End*, she wrote again. *The End, The End, The End,* she typed over and over, bitterly disappointed that this hadn't somehow made her mother reappear.

'It's no good,' Tuesday said in frustration. 'It's not working.'

'Hrrrr,' said Baxterr sympathetically.

Tuesday sat and thought.

'Who wants to start at The End?' she said to Baxterr. 'Maybe what we need is a beginning.'

She unrolled the page from the typewriter and turned it over, so she had a completely blank page again. Then she began. The words appeared rather slowly because she wasn't used to typing and had to keep looking for the right keys, but this is what she wrote – *One dark starry night when all the city was sleeping, a girl and a dog waited by an open window.*

As Tuesday typed, something strange happened. While the words appeared in nice black letters on the page, as words do if you are typing, a silvery thread appeared with every word, just as if it were made of the very same thread as the words in the little silver case. They grew a little bigger, the silver words, as they took to the air and wrapped themselves carefully around Tuesday's left wrist. They felt cool and tingly against her skin.

'Baxterr,' whispered Tuesday, 'this is most unusual.'

Baxterr cocked his head and gave a curious little growl. 'Rrrrr.'

'Shh, you might frighten them,' said Tuesday.

The dog, Baxterr, Tuesday wrote, *was a fierce and fearless dog with a bushy tail.*

And this sentence too became floating silver letters that formed themselves into a strand. It joined up with Tuesday's first sentence and twined around her forearm, reaching up as high as her elbow.

Baxterr loved strawberry ice-cream, teriyaki chicken and steak tartare, wrote Tuesday. And this time when the silvery letters floated off the page and linked up with the others, they coiled up to Tuesday's shoulder, making her shiver as if tickled.

Baxterr growled again. 'Rrrr.'

In a rush she wrote—*Each morning Baxterr walked Tuesday to school. On Mondays, Tuesdays, Wednesdays and Thursdays, they walked home after school together.*

But although the silvery thread was stretching across the back of Tuesday's neck and down her right arm, her sentence wasn't quite long enough for the words to reach all the way down to her right wrist, so Tuesday turned the full stop into a comma, and added—*usually stopping to play frisbee in the park*—which almost did the trick—*and buy liquorice allsorts*—which wasn't the least bit true, but the silvery letters were encircling the fingers of her right hand and drifting towards her middle.

But on Fridays, she continued, *Tuesday and Baxterr flew home, because Baxterr was a magic dog with magic wings.*

Still, the typewriter was producing two kinds of words—the black ink ones that were staying on the page, and the silver thread-like ones. She typed faster and faster: *Tuesday had always thought it was lovely to have a magic dog with magic wings, but a day came when it was more than just lovely. It was essential. Because on this particular day Tuesday had discovered that her mother was missing and although her father (who was wise about many things) said she would soon be back, Tuesday felt sure that something terrible had happened. Wherever her mother was, she must be in need of help and it was up to Tuesday, and Baxterr, to find her and bring her home.*

The thread looped once, twice, thrice around Tuesday's chest and she was feeling quite light-headed, as if she had spun around on the lounge room carpet several times. Soon the letters cocooned her, growing larger and brighter.

Tuesday continued to type, her eyes fixed on the page: *The tricky part was knowing where to find her mother. Tuesday had only two clues. 1: her mother had left the window open. 2: her mother had left two words—The End—in a silver box on her desk. Tuesday knew that although the story her mother was writing was very nearly at The End, it wasn't quite there yet.*

'That was it!' Tuesday thought. Her mother must be stuck, somewhere near The End, wherever that was. The more she thought about it, the more she felt sure that this was exactly what had happened: her mother was having trouble at The End. Everyone knew it was hard to begin a story, but much harder to actually finish one.

At that moment a long silver thread snaked upwards as if it wanted to pull Tuesday into the air. She pulled it back and tucked it firmly into her pyjama pocket, then continued typing. She wrote: *But just as Baxterr was no ordinary dog, Tuesday was no ordinary daughter. She was determined to find her mother, no matter what it took.*

There was no mistaking it. Tuesday was in a swirl of silver threads so fine and sparkly that it was like being inside spun toffee and she was lifting up out of the chair. Her feet were off the ground and she was rising up, up, up.

'Oh, Baxterr,' Tuesday giggled. 'Look at me! I'm taking off!'

Baxterr barked loudly. Tuesday twisted and turned, gasping at the novelty of floating above her mother's desk.

'I'm flying. I'm really flying,' she said in wonder. 'Oh, Baxterr, don't just bark. Jump! Jump!'

And in a moment of moonlight and silvery letters in a room full of books all higgledy-piggledy, Baxterr took an enormous leap right up into Tuesday's arms.

'Tuesday!' came her father's voice, and there was Denis McGillycuddy, standing at the doorway in his tartan dressing gown.

'Tuesday, come down from there,' he called.

But Tuesday felt deliciously happy, as if she'd just jumped into a swimming pool on a hot afternoon. Baxter was panting in her arms as if he too felt the delicious, giddy feeling that was sweeping over Tuesday. He did not appear the least bit worried about floating with Tuesday towards the open window.

'We're going to find Mum,' Tuesday said to Denis.

'Oh, dear,' said her father. 'I saw it coming, but I didn't expect it quite so soon.'

'What?' Tuesday asked.

'Don't you see?' he said. 'You're off! You're off! A story has got hold of you. There's no denying the undeniable, no dilly-dallying with the un-delayable. Off you go then! Follow the words, my love, that's what a writer does. Just follow the words.'

'But *I'm* not a writer,' Tuesday called to him.

She and Baxterr were pulled gently over the windowsill by the thread. She could see the streetlights on Brown Street far below. She turned back and saw her father pluck her page of writing from the typewriter and examine it.

He nodded and called out, 'Oh, I think you are, my love. I think you truly are. But you mustn't stop. Keep on!'

Her father and the window grew smaller and smaller as the thread drew Tuesday and Baxterr on, away from the house and up into the sky. Denis McGillycuddy called out one more time.

Tuesday couldn't be sure, but she thought he said, 'Blueberry pancakes for breakfast!' Then she turned towards the silvery thread that stretched out as far as the stars ahead of her. She smiled, and let the air rush over her.

If you had been watching from where Denis McGillycuddy stood, then what you would have seen is this: a girl and a dog disappearing, as if a door had opened and then closed in the vast darkness of the night sky.

Chapter Three

All at once, there was nothing but night. Tuesday's house was nowhere to be seen. With a shiver of fear, Tuesday realised that Brown Street itself had disappeared, as had City Park, and her school too, and indeed the entire city in which she had spent her life so far. She was swimming in darkness.

An enormous moon lit up remnants of cloud, and stars that were bigger and brighter than she had ever known stars to be blinked in the endless black. It was very quiet other than a low, rushing noise as she and Baxterr were swept along behind the silver thread. The giddy feeling that had gripped Tuesday as she had been lifted into flight was evaporating, and Tuesday was beginning to worry about the fact that she was drifting high in a night sky with nothing more than a string of shimmering words and silvery sentences to keep her aloft. Baxterr planted a reassuring lick on her cheek, then turned his face into the breeze with the same expression of blissful freedom that he had whenever he stuck his head out of the car window.

If Baxterr wasn't afraid, Tuesday thought, then perhaps she ought not to be afraid either. Maybe, her mother did this all the time. Perhaps, on those occasions when Tuesday had believed her mother to be curled up in her red velvet chair, Serendipity had actually been up here, flying away to ... *where*?

There was no doubt that this was an adventure, Tuesday thought, and it occurred to her that she hadn't any first-hand experience in real adventures. All the adventures she had ever been part of had been with characters in books. She'd never actually had to scale towering cliffs or fight ferocious pirates or take a flying fox across a gaping ravine. She didn't like snakes and she certainly couldn't use a sword. She could swim, but she'd never tried to swim a rushing river. She couldn't shoot an arrow from a bow and she'd never sailed a boat or even caught a fish. It was very hard to learn any of the things you needed for an adventure when you lived in a city. The one thing she could do was run quite fast. She usually finished second or third in the school races. That might come in handy if she had to run away from danger. Although she wasn't sure running away was going to be much use in getting her mother back from wherever she was stuck. She might have to be braver than that.

Soon Tuesday was approaching a vast cloud shaped like a moonlit lake. It was dark at the edges, but light was spilling from the middle. As they flew closer Tuesday could see that in the centre of the lake of cloud was a small green hilltop with a single broad leafy tree. The thread of silver words stretching ahead was diving down towards the tree. It was as if the tree below had caught the long thread and was reeling Tuesday and Baxterr in like fish on a line.

In hardly any time at all they made landfall. Tuesday tumbled onto the grass beside Baxterr, who came to rest gracefully on all four paws. Hanging from the tree's branches, just above Tuesday's head, was her silver string. It rolled itself swiftly into a neat and compact ball that fell into her outstretched palm. It looked, now, like an ordinary ball of silver twine. She took a length of it between her hands and tugged. It was quite strong.

Tuesday looked around. All there was to see was the tree, and a hilltop covered in green grass and tiny white daisies. Whatever lay beyond was obscured by cloud. Tuesday examined the tree more closely. It seemed to her to be very old indeed. She walked a circle around its amazingly broad trunk, but she did not find her mother sitting up against it with her notebook in her hand. She peered up into the tree's wide and gnarly branches, but her mother was not perched among them.

It was very quiet, as if Tuesday and Baxterr were the only people in the universe.

'Hello?' Tuesday called out. 'Mum?'

No answer came, not even an echo of Tuesday's own voice.

'Hello? Hello? Mum?' Tuesday called again.

Still no answer came. The tree's bright green

leaves rustled, whispering to each other in some leafy language that Tuesday did not understand.

Tuesday dropped the ball of thread, willing it to unravel and lead the way, but it fell to the ground. She nudged it with her foot, hoping that it would roll purposefully in one direction or another so that she might follow. But it simply sat there, glinting slightly in the pale light.

'What do I do now?' she asked the thread as she picked it up and rolled it about in her hands. 'Follow the words. That's what Dad said. But how can I follow the words if they don't *go* anywhere?'

Tuesday looked to her dog for an answer, but he was busy sniffing out smells in the grass.

'Oh, I don't know what to do,' she moaned.

Then a single leaf floated free from the tree and twirled down in front of Tuesday's face. She caught it by its stem and flattened it out on her palm where she could examine it carefully. It was a heart-shaped leaf, and like every other leaf Tuesday had ever seen, it had little veiny lines on it. But unlike the little veiny lines on any other leaf, this leaf had lines that had arranged themselves into what appeared to be writing. It *was* writing! Tuesday peered closely. She had to squint to make out the words written on the underside of the leaf.

Begin, start, commence, set off, strike out, she read.

'Baxterr!' she called. 'Doggo, look at this. Maybe *these* are the words we're supposed to follow! *Begin, start . . .*'

But Baxterr's gaze was fixed on the sky. He gave a sharp bark as another silver strand of words appeared above them. It had been fashioned into a lasso, and it was whirling rapidly towards the tree. Tuesday instinctively ducked behind the tree trunk and called Baxterr to her. With her arm around his middle, she could feel how his little body was tensed up, ready to spring into action if necessary. The loop of the lasso circled an outer branch of the tree and pulled tight. A person streaked through the air at great speed, turned a tidy forward flip and landed on his feet.

'Yes!' he said, pumping the air with his fist. He looked to be only a few years older than Tuesday, a teenager with dark blond hair, long gangly legs and arms, and a wide, square face. He was wearing jeans, a t-shirt, runners and a backpack.

Peering cautiously around the tree, Tuesday watched as the boy attempted to free his lasso from the branch.

'C'*mon*,' the boy said, yanking at the thread, and at last, in a blur of silver, the thread wound itself into a ball, just as Tuesday's had done, though Tuesday noticed that the boy's ball of thread was much bigger than hers. The boy shrugged his backpack off and slipped the thread into one of its pockets. Evidently thinking himself to be alone, he then buried his index finger in one of his nostrils, picked out a bogey, and chewed it off the end of his fingertip. Tuesday pulled a face.

When she sneaked another look, the boy was facing the tree. Tuesday drew back, grateful for the size of the trunk. She wasn't sure why she was hiding, but it seemed like a good idea until she knew a little more.

'Action-packed thriller,' the boy said, as if he were speaking to the tree. 'Heroes, bad guys, radical plot twists, plenty of explosions.'

One of the tree's lower branches sprouted a russet-coloured pod that burst out into a weather-beaten leather jacket and a pair of commando-style boots. The boy sat on the other side of the tree and slipped off his runners. He struggled to loosen the laces of the enormous boots and wedge his feet inside.

'Couldn't you make them with Velcro?' he asked, as he got himself into an awful tangle involving the various holes and metal hooks that the laces had to be poked through and wound around.

After hearing this struggle go on for some minutes, Tuesday slipped from her hiding place.

'Would you like a hand with those?' she asked.

The boy looked up and stared at Tuesday, who found herself acutely aware that she was wearing pyjamas: her favourite cupcake pyjamas that she had mostly grown out of at the ankles and the wrists.

'It's just that I'm good with laces,' she continued, 'and you seem to be having trouble.'

The boy shook his head decisively.

'No way,' he said. 'I don't have *girls* in my books. Look, the dog maybe,' he said, eyeing Baxterr. 'But no *girls*. So, be off.'

He flicked his hand at Tuesday as if she were an annoying insect to be shooed away.

'I'm sorry, but I think there's been a misunderstanding,' said Tuesday. 'I don't want to be in your book.'

'Good,' said the boy.

He stood up, leaving his laces wound haphazardly about the tops of his boots.

'That will never do,' said Tuesday. 'You'll trip over. Sit down.'

To her surprise, the boy did sit down. Tuesday made short work of weaving the laces in the necessary crosswise pattern and finishing off with a sturdy double-knot.

'Hah. Thanks,' said the boy, looking down at the boots, pleased. 'So what *are* you doing here?'

'I'm looking for my mother,' said Tuesday, sitting down beside the boy. 'She didn't come home last night, you see. So I was fiddling with her typewriter, and then this silvery thread...'

Tuesday pulled her mysterious ball of thread out of her pocket, and the boy's eyes grew wide.

'What the ... you're a ... oh, I see. Hey,' said the boy uncertainly.

'Hey,' said Tuesday, not sure what the boy was saying.

His expression was curious, cautious even.

'What's your name?' he asked.

'Tuesday,' said Tuesday. 'Tuesday McGillycuddy.'

'Never heard of you,' he said suspiciously.

'Why should you have heard of me?' Tuesday asked, confused.

'Okay,' he said slowly. 'So this is your first time here, right?'

'Yes,' Tuesday confirmed.

The boy raised his eyebrows and gave an unfriendly little chuckle.

'Well, you've got a long way to go then,' he said. 'Just so you know, I'm Blake Luckhurst. *The* Blake Luckhurst,' he added, pointing a finger at himself.

His name did vaguely ring a bell, but Tuesday couldn't quite place it.

Seeing Tuesday's blank face he continued, 'First published at twelve. Million books sold by the time I was thirteen. Two films in the making. Jack Bonner—my hero—bestselling action figure last Christmas, in case you've been living on the moon.' Blake Luckhurst had a very annoying way of speaking as if having to converse with Tuesday at all was wasting both his time and his intelligence.

'Oh, so you're a writer,' said Tuesday, thinking out loud.

'Oh, Yesterday, you are so *fast*,' said Blake sarcastically. 'And I guess you're thinking of becoming a writer, too. Or is it him?' he snorted, pointing at Baxterr. 'Got a shaggy dog story, fella?'

Baxterr gave an offended *ruff* and cocked his head.

'It's Tuesday,' she corrected, in case he had somehow misheard her name, though she suspected he hadn't. Tuesday was used to being teased about her name, but she had learned that if she didn't get upset about the teasing it eventually stopped. 'And this is Baxterr,' she continued. 'As a matter of fact, neither of us is a writer. My mother is the writer, and we're here to find her.'

'Well,' said Blake, 'if you're lucky, your story might not completely suck. Meanwhile, I've got a publisher breathing down my neck, so I'm off to The End. Ciao, Yesterday.'

With that, Blake Luckhurst picked up his backpack and walked away.

'The End?' Tuesday asked, jumping to her feet and following him. 'I think my mother's at The End. You see, she's lost and I'm trying to find her. Could I come with you?'

Blake looked at Tuesday incredulously. 'Yeah, right,' he said, then strode away in earnest.

'Wait!' yelled Tuesday, racing down the hill after him. 'Blake, wait! Please wait!'

Baxterr, picking up the scent of a chase, hurtled downhill, overtaking Tuesday and barking excitedly. Just as Blake was about to step into the whiteness of the cloudbank ahead, Baxterr caught the ankle of his jeans neatly between his front teeth.

The boy shook his leg, trying to loosen Baxterr's grip on his trousers, but Baxterr only stared up at him stubbornly. Blake ran his fingers through his mop of blond hair and tried to smile at Tuesday, as if he thought that might help.

'C'mon, we're all friends here, Yesterday,' he said. 'Tell your dog to let go.'

'First tell me the way to The End,' said Tuesday fiercely.

'You don't know anything, do you?' said Blake.

Tuesday glared at him.

'Well, I know two things,' she said. 'You pick your nose and eat it, and you can't even tie your own shoelaces, so I don't know why you think you're so great.'

Blake Luckhurst's face reddened.

'Okay, fair enough,' said Blake in a softer voice. 'But it's like storytelling *kindergarten*—you can't get to The End unless you've been to The Beginning and The Middle. I mean, that's how books work.'

'Well, thank you for that illuminating insight into the basic structure of a story,' said Tuesday, 'but I don't *want* to write a story. I told you, I want to get to The End and find my mother because that's where she's stuck. Can you at least tell me—am I close? Is it far?'

'Yesterday,' said Blake, 'you're nowhere near The End. This hillside here, this is The Beginning.'

And suddenly Tuesday understood. She understood that she was in the place where stories happen because somehow she'd been mistaken for a writer. And she had no idea how to go on, or how to get back again. Just thinking about how far she was from home made Tuesday's throat tight and her eyeballs prickly. She gulped and blinked in a valiant attempt not to cry, but despite her very best efforts, one fat tear escaped from each eye and ran down her cheeks.

'Oh, no,' said Blake awkwardly. 'Boy, I am glad I never had sisters. Look, you can't cry. Not on your first day. It'll be all right. Really ... I mean, you've begun. Look at your thread. C'mon. You've done something that's incredibly hard to do. You got lift-off. Now you just have to go on.'

'But how?' said Tuesday, her voice quavering.

Blake sighed. 'Look, I've got a deadline, right? So this has to be quick. Listen up.'

Sensing things had changed, Baxterr released Blake's jeans.

'Sometimes,' said Blake, 'getting to The End can take years. Of course for me, it usually only takes eight to ten weeks at the longest.'

'Weeks?' Tuesday cried. 'I can't take *weeks*. I need to be home by breakfast.'

Blake sighed. 'Hey, chill. Time here and time at home are different. It's like, you know, Narnia. Sometimes you get home thinking you've been away for weeks, and you find no time has passed at all. Other times, you get home and realise you actually *have* been gone for days. That freaks people out, I can tell you.'

'Well, can I fly to The End the same way I flew here?' Tuesday asked hopefully.

'Nope,' said Blake.

'So, how *do* I get there?' Tuesday asked.

'Do what everyone does. Make it up as you go along. If you're good enough, you'll get there.'

'And if I'm not good enough?' Tuesday asked, frowning.

Blake flicked his fringe out of his face and shrugged nonchalantly.

'I've never had that problem.'

Tuesday felt tears gathering.

'Okaaaay,' said Blake, 'I don't think you're getting it.' He sighed. 'I'll take you to the Librarian. After that, I'm gone. Got it?'

'The Librarian? There's a library here?' Tuesday asked.

'Yep, one giant library. Right out of my way,' said Blake, 'but the Librarian would never forgive me if I left you here.'

He scrutinised Tuesday's pyjamas.

'You might want to get changed first.'

'Oh dear,' said Tuesday in a small voice. 'I didn't bring anything else to wear.'

Blake flicked his hand again. 'Talk to the tree. I'll wait over there. But hurry up.'

Blake strode away. Baxterr followed close at his heels with the clear intention of making sure Blake did not leave without taking Tuesday with him.

Tuesday hurried back to the tree. 'Hello,' she said in her politest voice. She felt silly talking to a tree, but she continued.

'I need ... um ...'

But what did she need? What clothing did you wear to go in search of a lost mother? If there were to be snow-capped mountains, then possibly she might need furs. If there were islands and beaches, she might need bathers and a large hat. If there were castles and royalty, then a ball gown might be more appropriate. Tuesday simply had no idea, but somehow she doubted that she'd need the ball gown.

'I'm sorry, but I have no idea what my journey might involve, so I'm hoping you might find me something appropriate,' she said.

The tree rustled its leaves, as if in a light breeze, and Tuesday's pyjama top changed into a blue t-shirt. Her pyjama pants transformed into a pair of faded blue cotton shorts that were already soft and comfortable. Tuesday squeezed her ball of silvery thread into a front pocket. Then she watched in delight as a branch of the tree sprouted a russet pod that rapidly unfurled into a red jacket; and then another bloomed into a backpack that was neither too big nor too small, but just the right size. She had nothing to put into it, but she picked it up anyway.

Then, out of a hollow in the tree shot a pair of emerald green shoes that were the same shade of green as the rollershoes lying beneath her bed, back in her house in Brown Street. But since these shoes had no wheels in the heels, Tuesday gathered that her journey was not going to be particularly smooth. Nevertheless, she slipped them on and tied the laces securely. They were a perfect fit and very comfortable.

'Thank you,' said Tuesday to the tree, which rustled its leaves a little more vigorously in response.

She hurried down the hill to the edge of the

cloudbank where Blake was waiting impatiently with a vigilant Baxterr watching over him.

'Stay close,' Blake said as he took a long stride into the misty whiteness.

Almost instantly he disappeared.

'Blake!' Tuesday called.

He reappeared.

'I said stay close,' he said.

'Could I hold your hand?' Tuesday asked. 'I can't see anything!'

'You really are pathetic, aren't you?' he said, but he grinned as he held out a hand that Tuesday took gratefully in hers. 'Don't worry. I've been here plenty of times so we won't get lost.'

'Okay' said Tuesday, and the three of them set off into the cloud.

The mist was not unpleasant to walk through. It was neither wet nor cold, and Tuesday fancied that it smelled faintly of cinnamon. The ground beneath her feet was a pathway of sorts, made of stone, and the path was wide enough for the three of them to walk side by side. Despite the thickness of the mist that if Tuesday were alone would have had her putting her hands out in front of herself and hoping she wouldn't run into anything, Blake strode along at a good pace.

'How do you know we're not going to fall off a cliff?' Tuesday ventured.

'Because, as I said, I've been here before. This will all look very … different … to you … next time.'

But there won't be a next time, Tuesday wanted to say. *Once I find my mother I'm going home and I'll never come here again.* But instead she concentrated on keeping up with Blake, and trusted he was keeping them on the path.

For a little while they strode along in silence. At last Blake said, 'So, Yesterday Mcwatchamacallit, who are your favourite writers?'

'Serendipity Smith,' Tuesday said, a little cautiously. 'Have you heard of her?'

'Heard of her? Are you serious? Of course I've heard of her,' Blake said condescendingly. And then, in quite a different tone, he said, 'And yeah, she's actually pretty cool.'

'Well, Serendipity Smith is …'

Baxterr gave a low growl and Tuesday stopped herself, just in time, from blurting out the secret that she'd kept, utterly and perfectly, for more than half her lifetime. She shook herself a little. What had she been thinking? Was it the strangeness of being here, the mist, the unreality of everything that had happened since last night that had made her for a moment almost blurt out the one thing she had sworn never to say?

'...my favourite author of all time,' she finished.

Never before had Tuesday wanted so badly to let the secret out. She had to clamp her lips together and catch her tongue behind her teeth. But Blake, who was a dark shape in the whiteness beside her, noticed none of this.

'Except for her endings,' said Blake. 'I mean, why is Mothwood still *alive*? If it were me, I would have iced him at the end of the first book. But, you know, that's just my style.'

Tuesday rolled her eyes. But she smiled, because even if Blake was irritating and arrogant, he was also holding her hand in the fog and taking her to the Library, and Tuesday felt certain that at last she was getting somewhere.

Chapter Four

And now we must return to Brown Street, where all the houses stood shadowed in the deepest dark of night.

Only one house, the tallest and narrowest on the street, showed any sign of activity. It might almost have been mistaken for a lighthouse, for while most of its windows were dark, the topmost window was brilliantly lit. It was as if someone was at work in there. But there was no one at work. There was no one in the room at all, and the only movement came from the deep red curtains that caught the moonlight as they drifted in and out of the window with each gentle breath of wind.

What happened next happened fast, and you would only have seen it if you had been watching extremely carefully. A thin strand of silvery thread slipped silently over the sill of the open window, and pooled on the honey-coloured floorboards. Swiftly, the thread gathered itself up, and spun itself into a ball. As more and more thread slithered into the room, the ball grew larger. At first it was the size of a golf ball. Then it was the size of a tennis ball, and finally—when the ball was almost as big as a grapefruit—the very end of the thread snaked over the sill. It was attached, quite firmly, to the hand of a slender, dark-haired woman, who glided in through the window and touched her feet down quietly on the floor.

Who was she? Why, it was none other than Serendipity Smith, the most famous writer in the world. Of course, she didn't look at all like Serendipity Smith. Her brown eyes were not framed by the most elaborate Lucilla La More spectacles. She wore comfortable black clothes, not a gorgeously tailored velvet coat lined with paisley silk. Her feet were clad in sensible black runners, not knee-high boots of the finest plum-coloured leather. But still, as you know, it was Serendipity Smith.

Serendipity stretched and sighed and yawned, rubbing her fists into her tired eyes. Pulling a pencil from behind her ear, she used its tip to scratch an almost unreachable itch on her back, then she turned her gaze to the ball of silvery thread, which lay, quivering slightly, at her feet. She scooped it up and placed it on her desk, beside her typewriter, then settled down at her chair.

From the pile of paper on the right-hand side of her desk, Serendipity took the top sheet and slid it into the typewriter. It was the same piece of paper to which Tuesday had tried to stick *The End* only a few hours before. Slowly, Serendipity began. *Click, clack*, went the keys of her typewriter. *Click, clickety, clack*. She gathered speed, the look upon her face changing with each new scene she described upon the page. Sometimes she smiled, and sometimes she scowled, sometimes she looked positively frightened, and for a while there, it looked as if she might cry.

When she had filled each page, Serendipity inserted a fresh sheet into her typewriter. And then another, and another. As the words appeared on the page, Serendipity thought back over the events of her long, long day. Had it truly been just that morning that Vivienne and Mothwood had fought their final battle? Page after page were filled as these two archenemies fought to the death. Mothwood had executed one final cruel trick, but his plan had backfired and he had tumbled to his death.

'Oh, Mothwood, my old foe,' Serendipity whispered.

Serendipity had thought, and indeed hoped, that perhaps the fifth and final book in the Vivienne Small series would *not* end with Mothwood's death. She had wanted to believe that even after all his evil deeds, maybe, just maybe, he was capable of something noble – heroic, even – that would redeem him. In the end, however, despite her best attempts to save him, Mothwood had proved himself a villain to the very core.

'Goodbye, Mothwood,' Serendipity said, as the words on her page told the story of his final moments. 'I shall miss you, vile as you have always been.'

She threaded one last page, on which she wrote the scene where Vivienne Small returned safely to her secret tree house in the Peppermint Forest, under cover of darkness. Finally, she came to the very last sentence: *Vivienne lay down in her hammock to sleep, although her right ear, the one with the pointed tip, remained tuned—as ever—to the call of adventure.*

Serendipity sighed. It was, she hoped, an ending that her readers would find satisfying. She rubbed her stiff neck and looked out the window into the darkness of the night. It was very, very late. It was so late that it was actually quite early. In just an hour or so the sky would lighten and birds would sing their morning songs. But she had done it. She had finished. She had finally written the last sentence of the last Vivienne Small book ever.

She checked her watch. It was Saturday morning and today was the first day of Tuesday's summer holidays. Eight whole weeks stretched out before them; weeks where Serendipity didn't have to write, or think about writing, or wear purple boots and long coats and pretend to live in an apartment on the top floor of the most famous hotel in the city. In a few hours she would rouse Tuesday from her bed. And then, at breakfast, Serendipity and Denis would surprise Tuesday with the news that tomorrow they would all be going to a tiny, ramshackle shack on the most remote island in the whole Pacific Ocean, where they could snorkel and sail every day. There would be just Serendipity and Denis and Tuesday and Baxterr. No book signings, no television appearances, no radio interviews, no literary festivals. Just reading and dreaming and snorkelling and sailing and playing Cluedo and Scrabble and cards.

Wearily, Serendipity reached for the silver case containing *The End*. Flipping open the tiny box, she was surprised to see that the words were not, as they usually were, laid out in their tidy, curling script. Instead they were all scrunched up and unreadable, as if they'd been blown about in the wind.

'That's very odd,' Serendipity said.

But, being too tired to give it any further thought, she simply lifted out the silvery thread and was about to place the words down at the bottom of her page, when she stopped.

'No, not yet,' she whispered. 'Best to sleep on it.'

For Serendipity knew what all writers know: that once *The End* has been set down at the bottom of a page, that's it. It's over. The story is absolutely, quite definitely finished. Serendipity told herself that she would return to her writing room later in the morning, after breakfast, and check over the manuscript one last time. And then, if she was happy, she could add *The End*. Yes, she decided, *The End* could wait until then. It was time to sleep.

Serendipity pulled the window closed, latching it securely. The ruby beads hanging from the lamp on the table tinkled as she switched it off. She flicked off the main light too, wondering vaguely who had left it on, and suspecting that Denis must have done this to welcome her home. The door clicked closed behind her and she padded quietly down the stairs.

But before she went to bed, there was something she had to do.

And perhaps you know what it is. Or perhaps you don't. Perhaps you don't actually know that long after you have drifted off to sleep, your mother or father or someone else who loves you will invariably tiptoe into your room. They will pull your covers up over your shoulders if it's cold, or fold them at the bottom of your bed if it's hot. They will turn your light down, or off, and pick up that pair of shoes you've left lying in the middle of the floor. And do you know what they do next? For the briefest moment, they will watch you sleeping. They might stroke your cheek, or kiss your head, or whisper a good dream into your ear. Or perhaps they just stand there and think how lovely you are, and blow you a kiss, and leave you to your sleep.

Like most mothers, Serendipity loved to look in on her daughter before she went to bed herself. And so, tired as she was after her long, long day, she had a gentle smile on her face as she tiptoed down the stairs to Tuesday's bedroom. As usual, Tuesday had gone to sleep with her light on, and her bedroom door ajar, so there was light spilling out of the room onto Serendipity's feet as she carefully pushed open the door. But what Serendipity saw was not at all what she expected to see.

In Tuesday's bed, there was no Tuesday. Instead, face down, half under the covers, in his dressing gown, and with his slippers still on, was Denis. Serendipity stared at him. Frowning, she slipped across the room and shook him. Denis's eyes flew open.

'What's happened?' Serendipity asked. 'Where's Tuesday?'

'Back already?' Denis said, coming slowly to his senses. 'How did it go? Did she find you all right?'

'Did *who* find me?'

'Well, Tuesday.'

'Tuesday!' said Serendipity, startled. 'Why on earth would Tuesday…'

'She went to find you,' said Denis, bewildered, his hair mussed, his hand searching about for his glasses on the bedside table.

'Find me? How could she possibly find me?' Serendipity said, starting to sound shrill. 'Why isn't she here with you?'

'Well, because, she went to find you,' Denis repeated, also starting to sound a little angry. He sat up, put on his glasses and looked keenly at his wife.

68

'But that's impossible,' said Serendipity, sitting down beside him. 'You know that's impossible.'

'Not if she started a story that would take her there,' said Denis.

'But she's a child. Surely, she couldn't…'

'But she did,' said Denis, a little more calmly. 'Here, look.'

And he drew from his dressing-gown pocket the story Tuesday had begun on the typewriter. He unfolded the single page and handed it to Serendipity, who slowly took in the words.

'And Baxterr?' she asked, when she had finished.

'With her.'

'There was nothing… different about him?' Serendipity asked, frowning.

'Not at all.'

'Oh my goodness,' said Serendipity. 'She really did it.'

'The only problem is,' said Denis, 'she's gone looking for you *there*, and now you're… *here*.'

They sat there together for a moment in silence, both staring at the sheet of paper. Then Serendipity jumped up and said, 'I have to go. I have to find her.'

Denis nodded. 'I think that might be best.'

'If I go quickly, maybe I can catch her before she gets to the Library. Once the Librarian gets hold of her, well ... then it'll be too late for her to back out. She'll have to go all the way to The End,' said Serendipity, starting for the door.

'All right,' said Denis, following her.

'I can't believe you let her go,' Serendipity said as they quickly climbed the stairs. 'Was there nothing you could do?'

'No,' said Denis. 'She was in the air by the time I got there. Before I'd even crossed the room she was out the window. Baxterr was in her arms, and she looked so entirely happy. They both did.'

'Oh dear, oh dear, oh dear,' said Serendipity. 'The first time can be very tricky, you know. Anything could happen.'

'She's a clever girl,' said Denis. 'She'll work it out.'

'I should have been back!' Serendipity said, her brow furrowed, her tone growing more anxious by the moment. 'But I felt such an urgency to finish the book. I'd never experienced anything like it. I had this enormous surge of determination that I *must* finish today. I never imagined ... '

Back in her writing room, Serendipity flung open the window and called hopefully, 'Tuesday! Tuesday!'

The empty sky made no reply, although an early morning jet passed high overhead with its wing lights blinking.

Chapter Five

'This is it,' said Blake Luckhurst, peeling his hand away from Tuesday's.

They were still surrounded by the mist that had been with them since they had left the hillside of The Beginning. Tuesday didn't think they'd been walking for very long, but it had been long enough for her hand to become sweaty holding onto Blake's. She wiped it discreetly on her jacket.

'The Library,' Blake announced, pointing.

As Tuesday watched, the mist rolled back to reveal two carved lions crouching on stone plinths. Tuesday followed Blake along the path and up wide stone stairs. She could hear a fountain trickling, but she couldn't see it. At the top of the stairs was an enormous building. At the entrance were polished wooden doors, and etched in enormous letters into the stone above these doors was a single word – *Imagine.*

'Yeah, yeah,' said Blake Luckhurst as he saw Tuesday taking in the word. 'As if anyone forgets *that.*'

He pushed open the doors to reveal a vast marble foyer with huge columns, wide corridors and many doorways. Standing just inside, waiting for them to enter, was an ancient woman. She was so short that she was smaller than Tuesday, and so old that her face was as lined as a walnut. Despite her age, she was sprightly and graceful. She wore a long lilac gown, and a short velvet jacket in the same shade, as if she were dressed for an evening at the opera. The lilac clothes enhanced the colour of her eyes, which were a deep, shining violet.

'Blake Luckhurst,' she said imperiously.

Although she was looking up at Blake when she said this, she managed to convey the impression that she was actually looking down on him. Tuesday glanced sidewards at Blake who, to her surprise, was blushing and fidgeting nervously.

'Back so soon?' the woman said. 'I wouldn't want to think these stories of yours were hastily done. Hmmmm?'

'Ummm,' said Blake.

'We shall see. And you've brought me a new recruit,' the woman said, turning her intense gaze on Tuesday.

'This is Tuesday McGillycuddy, Madame Librarian,' Blake said in a surprisingly polite voice. Tuesday blinked. He knew her name perfectly well, after all. 'She's writing a rescue book,' Blake continued a little uncomfortably, 'about a lost mother – and as she herself was lost, I thought it best to bring her to you.'

Tuesday stared at Blake. Were all boys his age like that, constantly changing their behaviour? But she had no more time to think about it because the Librarian, her face alive with delight, was saying, 'Well, welcome, Tuesday McGillycuddy, to the Library. It is my great pleasure to meet you.'

She offered her tiny hand to Tuesday and gave Baxterr a brisk pat on the head. Tuesday observed the Librarian carefully, noticing how her white hair sat short and tight on her head like a luminous swimming cap. From her earlobes dangled two enormous, shimmering pearls that wobbled as she spoke.

'Now, Blake, go and get yourself some breakfast while Tuesday and I take a tour around the shelves,' she said commandingly.

'Nah, I'm good,' Blake said. 'Deadline.'

'That's no excuse for going without breakfast, Blake Luckhurst. I won't hear of it. Off you go. Now!' she said, firmly indicating a door on the far side of the foyer.

'Okay, sure, Madame Librarian,' said Blake, obediently loping away.

Tuesday couldn't help but smile to see Blake being bossed about.

'Well, then,' said the Librarian, clasping her hands together and turning again to Tuesday. 'Shall we?'

As the Librarian led Tuesday towards grand double doors on the right side of the foyer, Tuesday looked back at the disappearing Blake.

'Thank you, Blake,' Tuesday called to him.

Blake raised his hand lazily in farewell without turning.

Tuesday felt a small sting of sadness and wondered if she would see him again.

'It was very nice of him to bring me here,' said Tuesday.

'Oh yes, Blake can be such a sweet boy,' said the Librarian. 'But let's talk about you, dear Tuesday.'

The double doors swung open to reveal the biggest room Tuesday had ever seen. It wasn't just big, this room, like an art gallery or a museum. This room was as vast as a sports stadium. If she tipped her head right back, Tuesday could just make out ornate patterns and paintings on the ceiling far above her. Hanging down on long golden cords were lamps with green shades illuminating rows and rows and rows of bookshelves that were spaced across the floor. And every shelf, reaching from the floor to the enormously high ceiling, was filled with books.

'Oh!' gasped Tuesday, feeling very small.

'In this room,' said the Librarian, waving her hands like a conductor commanding an orchestra, 'is every story ever written. Your own will grace these shelves one day.'

'But I'm not writing a ...' Tuesday began.

'Hush,' the Librarian interrupted, turning a fierce frown upon Tuesday. Then, just as quickly as her frown had appeared, it disappeared, replaced by a cheerful smile. 'Stories, stories and more stories. The whole rich world of human imagination in every language, for all time – it's all here. I shall take you on a tour!'

The Librarian's hands flew all about and her pearl earrings shimmered.

'I think we might begin over here, today. At the end of the alphabet, just for something a little different,' she said, pointing to a row on the far side of the Library. Beyond the windows, Tuesday could see that the mist had not cleared. There was nothing but endless whiteness. The Librarian clicked her fingers and a small platform with a railing rolled towards them. The Librarian stepped onto the platform.

'On!' she instructed briskly, and both Tuesday and Baxterr obeyed, stepping up beside her.

Then, to Tuesday, the Librarian said: 'Hold tight.' And to Baxterr, she said: 'Sit.'

As the platform rose from the floor without

help from anything that Tuesday could see, the Librarian patted Tuesday's hand.

'Rrrrr,' said Baxterr, in a surprised fashion as the platform lurched slightly under his paws.

Tuesday gripped the platform's railing tightly, and wedged Baxterr's body between her feet to keep him safe. When they were quite a way up, the Librarian smiled.

'Are you ready?' she asked, her violet eyes twinkling.

Tuesday nodded uncertainly. The platform slipped sideways and Tuesday grasped the railing with all the strength she could muster and clamped her legs tighter against Baxterr. The Librarian giggled and Tuesday, half in terror and half in excitement, giggled too. Baxterr joined in with a delighted *ruff*. They whizzed past shelves full of books, diving up and down as if the platform were a dolphin leaping gently over waves as an ocean of books rolled by.

'Oh, I do *love* books, don't you?' the Librarian asked, rather breathlessly, reaching out to caress the multitudinous volumes as they passed.

Tuesday caught sight of authors' names

beginning with z's and y's and even x's. At the far end of the room, they rounded the corner of the shelves and started back the way they had come, the names beginning with w's, v's and u's. Rounding another corner, they were into the t's and, at length, the s's. Tuesday was feeling giddy.

'I suppose you have a lot of Smiths,' Tuesday said.

'Hmmm, what's that, dear?'

The platform slowed to a crawl so that the Librarian could lean close to Tuesday.

'Smiths. You must have a lot of Smiths,' Tuesday repeated.

'Yes! Smiths! Some people say Smith is a common name, but of course that's wrong – it's a *famous* name!' the Librarian cried.

As she was speaking, Tuesday caught sight of a long stretch of books covered in blue fabric, each of them with the name Serendipity Smith embossed on the spine in gold letters. Tuesday felt comforted that here in the Library were each of the Vivienne Small books, as well as all the other books Tuesday's mother had written before Tuesday was even born. She tried to look more closely, but the platform sped up again as if the Librarian had put her foot on an invisible accelerator.

'Some people write just one book. Only one!' said the Librarian, her hands flying up in wonder. 'And some people write hundreds! Incredible!'

Off they went again at speed, up and down the shelves, through the ranks of the R's and Q's and the P's, the O's and the N's. Then, once again, the speeding platform slowed, and rose higher. At length Tuesday, the Librarian and Baxterr reached a shelf right up near the ceiling. Here, the platform came to a halt and hovered, though it rocked gently as it did so.

'There,' said the Librarian, gesturing proudly to a shelf full of books by people whose names began with Mc.

'What am I looking at?' asked a bewildered Tuesday.

'This is where your book will go,' the Librarian said. 'I like to show every new recruit where they will be shelved – I find it spurs them on to great things!'

'Ruff,' said Baxterr, who was feeling safe enough

to reach his front paws up onto the railing of the platform where he could sniff the books for himself.

'You are going to do me proud, Tuesday McGillycuddy,' the Librarian said.

'No, no. This is a mistake,' Tuesday said.

The Librarian's gaze grew frosty.

'Oh?' she said.

'You see, I'm not a writer,' Tuesday stammered. 'My mother is a writer. I used her typewriter and, well, I don't know how it worked, but it did.'

'Not *it*,' said the Librarian impatiently. 'You. YOU! It's not typewriters that write books. It's writers.'

'But that typewriter ... I think it thought I was my mother.'

'Your mother?'

'Well,' said Tuesday, awkwardly. 'She's, well ...'

Tuesday bit her lip. It was the second time in one day that she had desperately wanted to blurt out the secret of her mother's true identity. 'Lost ...' she finished lamely.

'Lost,' said the Librarian, eyeing Tuesday keenly.

'Yes,' Tuesday continued almost in a whisper, averting her eyes from the Librarian's piercing gaze. 'I've come to find her but ... I'm not a writer at all.'

'I can assure you, Tuesday McGillycuddy,' said the Librarian quietly, 'that you can't get here because of a *typewriter*. You came because you have a story inside you wanting to get out. What happened might *appear* to be magical, but the magic comes from nowhere but within you. It doesn't matter whether you write on a fancy laptop or an old typewriter or, for that matter, with a pen on a paper napkin. All of that is beside the point. The point is that stories want to be told. Stories have a power of their own and they choose their writers carefully. But you can't write a story until you've felt it. Breathed it in. Walked with your characters. Talked with them. That's why you come here. To live your story.'

Tuesday gulped, feeling horribly out of her depth.

The Librarian looked at her more softly.

'Only writers come here, Tuesday,' she said. 'I can't tell you how to write your story, or what it will be called. I know only that you have talent, and a story strong enough that it has brought you here. You're here a little earlier than some, but you're not the youngest who has come. Does that make you feel a little better?'

'A little,' said Tuesday.

'Excellent,' said the Librarian, taking a deep breath. 'Now I must ask you for your thread.'

'My… thread?'

'Yes, Tuesday. The thread that brought you here.'

Tuesday took her ball of silvery string out of her pocket. 'What does the thread *do*?' Tuesday asked as she looked at it again. She felt reluctant to let it go. 'What is it for, exactly?'

'It is what tells me, Tuesday dear, that you are a real writer. It is the means by which you arrive here, and that's all you need to know for now. Let me keep it safe for you,' the Librarian said, smiling.

'Safe? Safe from what, or who?' Tuesday asked, still keeping the thread firmly in her hand. Tuesday wasn't sure why she felt as she did, but she didn't want to give her thread to the Librarian.

'I have not always needed to insist on these precautions, Tuesday. But now it seems to have become necessary,' said the Librarian, holding out

83

her hand. 'The world is less certain. Or perhaps people are less certain. I can't be sure.'

Tuesday extended her hand, but still her fingers clung to the ball.

'I'm not going to keep it forever,' said the Librarian sweetly, but her gaze was steely. 'Goodness, child. You may collect it again when your story is finished. I'm sure you will finish it, won't you, Tuesday?'

Baxterr let out a small growl, and Tuesday stroked his head to calm him. Reluctantly she released the ball of thread into the Librarian's hand.

'Oh, good girl. Very good,' said the Librarian with obvious satisfaction, instantly slipping the ball away into the folds of her gown and offering Tuesday a dazzling smile as a reward for her compliance. 'Now, let's get you started, shall we?'

Without waiting for an answer, the Librarian, set the platform in motion once again. Following a rather circuitous route, it zipped sideways, whizzed along rows and around banks of shelves, taking the corners fast so that Tuesday, Baxterr and the Librarian were squeezed together, and then flung apart.

Tuesday glanced over the edge of the platform to the floor far below. She noticed that interspersed between the banks of shelves were rows of dark wooden desks. Each desk was topped with a small green-shaded desk lamp and matched with a comfortable chair covered in green leather. Sitting at some of the desks were people who appeared to be writing or quietly reading.

'Those people down there, are they ... writers?' asked Tuesday.

'Yes, dear,' said the Librarian, dropping the platform a little lower, and slowing its pace so Tuesday could see more clearly.

Could her mother be here, at the Library? Tuesday wondered. She craned her neck, peering along the rows of desks, but her mother was nowhere to be seen. There were several women, but two had grey hair, one was wearing an elaborate headscarf and one had a long auburn ponytail. Tuesday observed several men, too. One was wearing a colossal white cowboy hat. He looked very familiar to Tuesday, and she thought perhaps that she recognised him from one of the literary events she and Denis had attended while pretending to be fans of Serendipity.

'Do you know,' Tuesday began carefully, 'if Serendipity Smith ever comes here? I mean, it's just that, well, she's my favourite writer. I expect she's lots of people's favourite writer...'

The Librarian's face broke into a delighted smile.

'Serendipity *Smith*? Yes, of course! She likes to sit at one of those desks just over there, by the window. Oh, how I long to read that new story of hers. I simply adore Vivienne Small. If I'm not mistaken, the fifth volume must be very, very close to finished.'

Tuesday's hopes soared.

'So, she's been here... lately? I don't suppose she's here right now, is she?'

The Librarian's delighted grin diminished to a half-smile. She turned away from Tuesday and the green-shaded lights above flickered and stalled, the way the lights did back in Brown Street when a thunderstorm was on its way. No sooner had Tuesday registered this slight disturbance than it stopped, and the lights regained their composure, glowing steadily once again. The Librarian turned her face back to Tuesday.

'Your main concern, Tuesday McGillycuddy, is your own story, is it not?'

Tuesday had the distinct impression that she'd once more said the wrong thing, but if she had, the Librarian gave no further sign of it as she brought the platform slowly and gracefully back to the Library floor.

'Well, here we are then,' said the Librarian cheerily, snapping her fingers to indicate to Baxterr and Tuesday that it was time to step down.

'This way,' she said, as she briskly led them out of the vast room. Tuesday blinked and looked back at the closed doors. It was hard to believe that such a vast room could actually exist, but she had no time to think about this because from the pocket of her lilac jacket, the Librarian had produced a large gold coin that she pressed into Tuesday's hand.

'You'll need this. Now, breakfast is through that door over there,' she said, pointing straight ahead in the direction she had sent Blake. 'The coin is not for the food, though. The food here is free, and the helpings generous, since I do not recommend that anyone attempt to write on an empty stomach.'

'Wait, though,' Tuesday began, 'about my mother...'

'Breakfast,' the Librarian said. 'And then, if I have time, I shall come and find you on the balcony. Oh, and by the way, I say this to all first-timers but they are prone to forgetting, so do please remember this. *Whether or not you can see it, the Library is always here.* All right? Now off you go.'

'All right,' said Tuesday, not understanding. 'But the coin – what *is* it for?'

'Goodbyyyieee,' sang the Librarian. And with that, she disappeared back into the great room of books, closing the doors behind her.

Tuesday sighed. She turned the coin in her hand and examined it carefully. It had a lion's head on one side and a mountain on the other and it appeared to be brand new.

Chapter Six

Through the doors the Librarian had indicated, Tuesday found a room that could easily have been a restaurant in a fancy hotel in the city. The tables were all set with white tablecloths, white plates, glassware and silver cutlery. Some of the tables were occupied; by writers, Tuesday assumed. Each of them sat alone. Some of them had a book propped open on the table while they ate, or a notebook that they were busily scribbling in. Several of them were simply staring out the window across the wide balcony beyond, with their spoon or fork halted in mid-air between their plate and their mouth. None of them took the least bit of notice of Tuesday or Baxterr.

Tuesday spied Blake Luckhurst at a table by the windows. As she approached, she saw that he was attacking an enormous pile of bacon. From the discarded plates piled on his table, she gathered this was not the first course of his meal.

'Hey,' said Blake, as Tuesday approached.

'Is it okay if I sit with you?' Tuesday asked.

Blake replied with a grunt.

'How do we order?' Tuesday said, sitting down opposite him. There didn't seem to be any waiters. Tuesday waited for Blake to reply, but he only continued forking bacon into his mouth. Tuesday had to admit that the bacon did look, and smell, particularly good.

'It's all very confusing,' she said. 'I came looking for my mother, but I still have no idea where to go, and now it seems I must have breakfast before I go anywhere.'

'Over there,' Blake indicated, waving his arm in the direction of a long buffet at the back of the room.

There were glass jugs of milk, three kinds of

juice and a row of silver domes. In front of each dome was a thick white card bearing words in elegant black writing. At the breakfast buffet of a fancy hotel, those cards might have announced veal sausages or baked beans or pancakes or scrambled eggs. But here they said things such as:

Confidence Food
It's Going To Be A Very Long Day
I'll Be Home By Lunchtime
I Eat Like A Sparrow
I Could Eat A Horse

and

I'm About To Get Myself Into Trouble

Then there was a basket at the end with a card that read:

Food For The Road

Tuesday lifted the silver domes to discover all manner of food. Under the lid of I'll Be Home By Lunchtime she found a ruby grapefruit and two slices of toast with marmalade. Under I'm About To Get Myself Into Trouble she found a plate of scrambled eggs, bacon, hash browns, tomatoes, sausages and waffles. At the end, she stopped at the basket of Food For The Road. Inside were a variety of packets. These were filled rolls and sandwiches, dried fruit and nuts, chocolate bars, cookies and apples in shades of red and green. Tuesday glanced over at Blake, but he had his head down over his food and was paying no attention to her.

She chose a roll filled with silverside and mustard, and then, thinking of Baxterr, she took a second roll. She selected a large chocolate bar for herself, and a packet of cheese and biscuits for Baxterr. She stuck these in her backpack along with two bottles of water. Then she went back along the sideboard to Confidence Food and lifted the lid. Underneath, on a blue-patterned plate, were two eggs, poached, on an English muffin with hollandaise sauce and bacon. It was exactly like Denis McGillycuddy's Monday morning breakfast, so she took a plate. Hearing Baxterr whine beside her, she lifted up the lid of I'm About To Get Myself Into Trouble and took a plate from there, too. Rather loaded up, she returned to the table where Blake Luckhurst was licking his knife. She placed the I'm About To Get Myself Into Trouble plate on the floor and Baxterr devoured the contents before she had even started on her first egg. Meanwhile, Blake leaned back on his chair and surveyed her.

'So, did she give you a coin?' he asked in a rather smug tone.

Tuesday wondered what had happened to the friendly boy who'd helped her through the mist. It seemed that he had evaporated and the annoying person she'd met at The Beginning had returned.

'Yes,' replied Tuesday mildly. 'What's it for?'

'Was I ever this dumb? No, Yesterday, I don't think I ever was,' Blake said, rolling his eyes. 'Whatever,' he continued, and stood up. 'I'm out of here.'

'Wait!' Tuesday protested. 'Couldn't you just stay for a minute?'

She had wanted to ask him about all kinds of things, not least about the ball of thread that the Librarian had insisted Tuesday leave in her care.

'It's a big world out there,' said Blake, pointing

to the balcony where Tuesday noticed a row of mounted binoculars fixed to the railings at various intervals, like the ones at tourist attractions. 'So you'd better start getting your head around the fact that there's only person here who can help you. And that's you. *Sayonara, sister.* Or, should I say, *hasta la vista, baby.*'

With that he picked up his backpack and loped through the restaurant and out the door, leaving Tuesday alone with the greasy remains of his breakfast.

'Fine,' she muttered and patted Baxterr's head. 'I feel like Alice in Wonderland. I've imagined six impossible things before breakfast, and now I know what happens when you do. You get very hungry.'

Tuesday finished her eggs. Then she neatly stacked her dishes, along with Baxterr's, and returned them to an empty spot on the buffet. Feeling for the coin in her pocket, Tuesday examined it again. She thought of approaching one of the writers at the other tables, but it didn't seem polite to disturb people who were clearly so preoccupied with their own thoughts. Tuesday glanced again at the misty balcony. She wondered if the coin had anything to do with the tourist binoculars. Calling Baxterr to follow her, she made her way out into the foggy surrounds.

'What do you think, doggo?' she asked Baxterr. 'Shall we get a closer look at this mist?'

Tuesday selected a pair of binoculars and located the coin slot behind the eyepieces. She slid her coin into it and turned a handle so that the coin clattered down inside the machine's workings. She looked, but just as she'd expected, there was nothing to see but whiteness.

'I don't know what to do,' Tuesday said to Baxterr.

'Ruff,' said Baxterr, as if he thought it was obvious what she should do.

Well, Tuesday thought, perhaps it was obvious. Binoculars were a device for looking, and she was indeed looking for something: her mother.

She peered again through the binoculars and was surprised to see the mist clear a little. She could see a wide sea and dark jagged cliffs, and a ship sailing towards her out of a storm. But it was no ordinary ship. It was huge and rusted with green moth-eaten sails. It was *The Silverfish*, the most feared vessel on the sea, captained by the villainous Carsten Mothwood.

Tuesday looked closely at all those on board the ship, but she could not spot her mother.

Tuesday pulled back from the binoculars and blinked. Taking a deep breath, she looked through them once again. Everything was shifting and moving. The mist was clearing and the sun was hovering at the edge of a deep pink dawn sky. She could see a forest—a tall, dark forest—and far beyond that was a glimpse of the sea, but it wasn't dark and wind-whipped as before. She realised that she knew that forest. She knew it almost as well as she knew the landscape of City Park. It was the Peppermint Forest, home to Vivienne Small.

Tuesday once again pulled back from the binoculars, and opened her eyes in wonder. It was as if a wind had blown, although none had, and the deep mist around the Library had dissolved. Beyond the balcony was the world she had seen through the binoculars, as if it had always been there. The sun *was* rising out of a deep pink dawn.

Far away to her left *was* the Peppermint Forest, a dark green mass beyond rolling fields. Beyond that and stretching all the way south was the Restless Sea, a shimmering expanse of cornflower blue tinted with silver.

'Oh,' Tuesday cried. 'Look! Baxterr, can you see that? I just know we're going to find Mum somewhere out there!'

Baxterr pushed his nose through the balcony railing. His tail wagged frantically and he barked in great excitement.

'Not bad,' came a voice beside Tuesday. 'Not bad at all, for a first try.'

Tuesday spun around. The Librarian was standing at the railing beside her and peering out over the landscape that had materialised around them.

'Did I ... do that?' Tuesday asked, stunned.

'Yes, dear,' said the Librarian calmly. 'The power of the imagination is a magnificent thing. Here, whatever you can imagine, you can make real.'

'It's amazing,' said Tuesday.

Beyond the railing, a curving staircase led steeply down into this strange and beautiful world.

Tuesday could hardly wait to get going. But the Librarian reached out a small hand and grasped Tuesday firmly by the wrist.

'There's one small problem with this world that you've made, is there not, Tuesday McGillycuddy?'

'Problem?'

'Unless I am very much mistaken, this world is not *yours*, is it? By my infallible recollection, this is the world of Vivienne Small—a world created by one Serendipity Smith.'

'Yes, but...'

'You've expressed an interest in Ms Smith's works, but I'm sure you know that your story needs to be *original*. Though I must say that I'm rather astonished,' the Librarian continued. 'I have never before seen a writer so vividly conjure up the world of another writer. Miraculous.'

Tuesday wished that she could tell the Librarian exactly why she should be able to perfectly imagine this world. She'd had Vivienne Small stories read to her all her life. She could picture every facet of the world down to its tiniest detail.

'I simply cannot have you dashing off into some other writer's world,' the Librarian continued sternly. 'What if Serendipity Smith were to come back and find some other writer meddling in her story? I cannot answer for the consequences if you intrude into the world of another writer! And I don't imagine you'd like it if I allowed anyone to go stomping around in a world of your creation now, would you? Hmmm?'

'But...' said Tuesday.

'No "buts". I will tolerate no "buts".'

'But...' said Tuesday, almost bursting with the desire to explain to the Librarian that she simply had to go into that world, and no other, because that was where she would find her mother. That she, Tuesday, had been present when her mother had created this world. That there had been times when her mother had asked Tuesday for ideas about how Vivienne Small could possibly escape her latest predicament and several of these ideas were in the Vivienne Small series. But how could Tuesday tell the Librarian any of this without revealing the secret that she was the daughter of Serendipity Smith?

Then, from across the balcony, came the sound of thumping, followed by a torrent of curses uttered in a thick Texan accent. The man in the white cowboy hat that Tuesday had seen working at a desk in the Library was standing at one of the other sets of binoculars, banging it with his fist in frustration.

'Madame Librarian,' he called out. 'What in tarnation! It done swallowed my coin!'

'Silver Nightly! Would you kindly stop mistreating my binoculars,' the Librarian said sternly.

But the man in the white hat took no notice. He retrieved a book from the pocket of his grubby white coat and used it to give the binoculars another hearty thwack.

'That is a Library book!' the Librarian screeched, setting off at a trot to rescue the book and the binoculars.

'Dang thang's plumb broke,' the man continued. 'Shoot, Madame Librarian, s'bout time you got these sorry antiquities replaced.'

Tuesday winked at Baxterr. 'What can she do to stop us, doggo?' she whispered.

Baxterr blinked and twitched his ears before quietly scampering off along the balcony away from the Librarian and the irate cowboy. Tuesday followed silently. In a few moments they had reached the staircase that descended into the world of Vivienne Small and Carsten Mothwood. As they began running down the stairs, Tuesday heard the Librarian above calling her name.

'Come on, doggo,' Tuesday urged him, 'faster!'

Nothing was going to stop her from finding her mother. Nothing and no one.

The staircase wound down and down and Tuesday and Baxterr didn't stop until they arrived at the last of the great stone steps and saw the land spread out before them. Tuesday's mind boggled with the extraordinary possibilities before her. She closed her eyes, threw her head back and smelled the air. It was just as she had always imagined—crisp and cold and fresh and ever so faintly minty. She bent down and brushed her hands over the long grass, which was greener than any grass she had ever seen. It was a truly deep green, and a little iridescent as well. Yellow flowers blooming out of the grass were as dazzlingly yellow as the grass was green, and the dawn sky overhead was giving way to royal blue with three long high clouds. It was the most beautiful place that Tuesday had ever been. She was astonished and amazed, and yet not surprised at all.

'Look, Baxterr!' she cried, pointing excitedly. 'That's the River of Rythwyck! And way over there, on the far side of the Restless Sea—those are the Mountains of Margolov. And there—there is the Peppermint Forest. If anyone can tell us how best to go on, and the quickest way to The End, then it's Vivienne Small. Mind you, I have no idea if she'll be home. Who knows what might have happened in *Vivienne Small and the Final Battle*. But if she is home, she is the one person who can help us find Mum. And if she's not there, she may have left a clue about where Mum might be. Imagine that, Baxterr—we might be about to meet the real Vivienne Small!'

Tuesday turned to take a last look up at the Library, only to find it had vanished. There were only high green hills that stretched all the way up the sky. With a little sting of fear, Tuesday realised how far she was from any place—or anyone—that she knew. Had she made a terrible mistake entering her mother's world against the Librarian's wishes? And how would she ever get back to it? How would she reclaim her ball of silver thread? *Whether or not you can see it, the Library is always here,* the Librarian had said, and Tuesday supposed she would simply have to believe that this was true. At that moment Baxterr gave a sharp bark and his body quivered.

'What's the matter, doggo?' Tuesday asked. But Baxterr continued quivering. Then he barked and took off at a trot, indicating to Tuesday to follow him.

'Baxterr? Baxterr! Come back!' Tuesday called.

Baxterr stopped long enough for Tuesday to catch up, then he barked sharply again as if to tell her that something was terribly wrong.

'Is it Mum? Is it Vivienne?' Tuesday asked, trying to soothe him.

But Baxterr barked again urgently and set off at a run towards the Peppermint Forest.

Chapter Seven

Meanwhile, back at Brown Street, Serendipity Smith sat down on the chair at her desk.

'Do you know how rare it is to get lift-off the very first time you try?' she said to Denis, her eyebrows scrunched together in a deep frown. 'If I wasn't so worried, I'd be incredibly proud of her. But there's so much she doesn't know. So much that could happen.'

'Perhaps I should have grabbed her leg and pulled her back in,' said Denis. 'But I was so happy for her. I didn't expect you to miss one another. I expected you both home for breakfast.'

'Well, we shall be, with any luck,' said Serendipity.

She inserted a fresh sheet of paper, and began. Under her fingers, the keys rattled and clicked. But although she willed the words to wisp up into long silvery tendrils that would wrap around her and take her away, they didn't. They stayed, black and blunt, on the page. There was no lift-off. None at all.

Serendipity ripped the page out of the typewriter, crumpled it up and threw it impatiently into the bin under the desk. She inserted a second fresh page, and began again, typing as fast as ever in her life. But still, she stayed glued to her chair.

'It's not working! I can't get any … lift,' she said. Serendipity felt a tide of panic rising.

'What do you need?' Denis asked.

'A beginning,' Serendipity said.

'What kind of beginning must it be?'

'It must be the beginning to a story that ends with a daughter being found. But it must be intriguing and interesting, or it will never fly.'

'Once upon a time … ?' Denis offered. 'A story can still begin that way, can't it?' he asked.

'Yes,' whispered Serendipity.

'Well then,' continued Denis, 'once upon a time

there was a child. A delicious, delectable, dear, darling daughter. How am I doing?'

'Hmmm,' said Serendipity, frowning a little.

'Oh, you know I'm no good at this.'

'Never mind that now. Just go on. Help me.'

Denis continued, 'She had golden hair and blue-green eyes, never was rude and never told lies.'

'I'm not sure…' said Serendipity.

'Rhyming's not right, is it?' Denis asked.

'But I think there's something in it,' said Serendipity.

And then her fingers reached for the typewriter keys and she tapped away.

Once upon a time a child was born on a Tuesday. She had eyes the colour of the ocean and feet as smooth as marble, with not a line or crease upon them.

'Ah,' said Denis. 'And then a bad fairy put a spell on her?'

'I'm not sure we need a bad fairy,' murmured Serendipity.

Serendipity continued crafting the story of Tuesday's first days in the world. But no matter how much Serendipity typed, how fast her fingers flew across the keys of the typewriter, how many ideas swam into her head, or how quickly Denis offered new thoughts and memories, no words curled up off the page. No silvery threads swirled about. She tried harder and harder, and discarded page after page, beginning again and again. Denis recounted the first word that Tuesday had spoken at nine months ('Up!') and the first word she had written in the sand at the beach aged two ('Up!'), and Serendipity remembered the first story Tuesday had brought home from school when she was in kindergarten ('The Girl Who Flew Up').

But nothing they thought of was enough to catch Serendipity up and fly her out the window into the sky that was pale with dawn.

'We can't. We're not allowed,' whispered Serendipity at last.

'What do you mean?' Denis whispered back, though nobody could hear them.

'I think that this is her story and she's going to have to find her way through it alone,' said Serendipity.

'Will she be all right?' Denis asked, peering out the window. 'What age were you when you first…?'

'About the age that Tuesday is now.' Serendipity smiled uncertainly.

'Then she'll be fine,' Denis said reassuringly, putting his arms around his wife and leading her to the windowsill. 'Who knows what adventures our girl might be having right now?'

'Yes,' said Serendipity, looking anxiously into the sky. 'That's precisely what worries me.'

Chapter Eight

Deep in the Peppermint Forest, the creatures of the night had returned to their burrows, nooks and nests to rest. Other forest inhabitants were shaking themselves awake and clearing their throats. Soon, the air would ripple with birdsong and the forest would take on the soft green glow of daytime. Fronds would unfurl, small footprints would appear on damp pathways, worms and caterpillars would begin their steady progress along stems of grass or the branches of trees. Spider webs would catch the first light, and maybe an early morning fly for breakfast. But in one particular towering, ancient peppermint tree, someone had no intention of waking up.

Every tree in the forest was beautiful in its own special way, but this particular tree held a house high in its broad branches. It was a small, octagonal house surrounded by a wide verandah. It had oval windows and a thatched roof. The woven timbers of the verandah railings were intertwined with a red creeper that attracted the attention of brightly coloured butterflies. From the verandah, suspended walkways disappeared off between other trees and into the forest canopy.

Lying in a hammock slung from the branches above, Vivienne Small was sleeping with her blue wings folded beneath her. Her hair was wild, dark and curly, held back from her face with a circlet of plaited leather. Her right ear, but not her left, was pointed like an elf's. Except for the fact that she was very small, about half the size of an ordinary girl, she looked the way girls look when they're asleep – that is: mostly harmless and somewhat unkempt. If her eyes had been open, you would have seen that they were grey-green, and capable of looking completely ferocious.

And if her wings had been extended, you would have seen that they were more like the wings of a bat than those of a butterfly, since they were jagged and leathery.

Vivienne had gone to bed just a few hours before, still wearing her knee-high boots, though she had taken the time to loosen their laces. Her face was smudged with what might have been soot, but was in fact gunpowder, and her hands were covered in scratches from a desperate climb.

It was unlike Vivienne to sleep in, but she had come to the end of a particularly long and gruelling adventure only the day before. Her elbows and knees wore the savage grazes that she had sustained during her final battle with Carsten Mothwood, and her chest and back were blotchy with bruises. Her ribs ached, one wing was painfully torn, and she had a colossal bump on the back of her head. She flicked one hand at the air beside her ear, as if to brush away an annoying, buzzing fly. But the sound that had woken her did not go away. Vivienne's pointed right ear had discerned the thud of a heavy footfall on the forest floor. The noise echoed through the roots of the trees and rustled up through the leaves. She opened her eyes and leapt out of her hammock, wincing at the pain in her ribs and her wing. She heard the snapping of twigs, the crushing of leaves and the toppling of toadstools as feet pummelled the earth. Vivienne sniffed and her nose filled with the unmistakable smell of revenge.

'Mothwood's men, blast them,' Vivienne said under her breath.

After the final defeat of Mothwood, Vivienne had made her way home across the Restless Sea in her little sailboat *Vivacious*. As she had rounded the last point into Nautilus Cove – the closest landing point to her tree house – she thought she had glimpsed a small, shadowy boat pursuing her in the moonless night. But she had been so utterly exhausted that she had dismissed it as a phantom of her imagination, and continued on her way home.

'Followed! How could I have been so careless?' she whispered crossly.

Vivienne made her way noiselessly around her tree house, making preparations. She filled a quiver with turquoise-feathered arrows, slipped the strap of the quiver over her shoulder and leaned her bow against the verandah railings in readiness. She fetched her Lucretian blowpipe and strapped a pouch full of poisoned darts around her waist. She peered over the railing, down through branches and plumes of leaves. Mothwood's men had circled the base of her tree. There were eight of them. Vivienne cursed herself again for being so careless. After years of infinite trouble to keep her tree house concealed, she had let its location be known.

'Vivienne Small!' called a pirate with a skull tattooed across his face.

Her only reply was to take careful aim.

'This is for Mothwood!' the pirate roared.

No sooner had he buried the sharp head of his axe into the trunk of the tree than Vivienne's arrow sped towards him, weaving through the branches and leaves, striking the pirate through his thick neck.

Whooping and laughing gave way to cries of outrage and fury as the pirate dropped to the ground. His comrades swung their axes in unison, metal biting into ancient timber. But Vivienne Small was not overly concerned. The tree was enormous and the timber of its trunk was as hard as iron, and there were only eight pirates below. She lifted her Lucretian blowpipe to her lips. With deadly aim, she let fly, and a dart buried itself deep in the eye of the pirate she had already wounded with her arrow. She watched as he fell instantly unconscious, the poison in her dart's tip coursing through his body. He would not wake until nightfall, and by that time, Vivienne would have him and his shipmates bound and safely deposited where they could do no further harm.

The remaining pirates roared in anger and redoubled their efforts, hacking at the tree trunk with all their might.

'For Mothwood!' they chanted, landing blow after blow.

The birds that had made their homes in the tree raised a chorus of disquiet, abandoning their nests and branches. The tree noted a mild vibration through its trunk and leaves, but remained unperturbed. Then, into the clearing, came another eight pirates. They were carrying a giant four-man saw. The tree shivered.

Vivienne lifted her bow in rage and fired at another pirate, then another and another. One she struck in the chest; another in the back of the neck. None of the fallen got up again but lay on the ground, howling in pain. Soon she would silence them all with her blowpipe, but first her arrows would work faster to disarm her attackers. She was about to release another turquoise-feathered bolt when she heard an ominous sound: the whoosh of wings beating the air.

Vivienne swung around, ready to release the arrow poised in her bow, but it was too late. Mothwood's enormous crow was upon her. He was the size of an albatross, with a gleaming black beak. He had wrinkled grey skin around his small black eyes and a body that was a mess of unkempt feathers and bald patches. He may have been almost three hundred years old, but this was a bird of uncanny strength and wit. Baldwin was his name, though Vivienne had another name for him.

'Bald One,' Vivienne Small hissed.

'Vivienne Small,' the crow shrieked as he fell upon her.

With his powerful beak, Baldwin grabbed Vivienne's bow, tearing it from her hands and flinging it away into the forest below. Vivienne reached for her blowpipe, snatching a new dart from the pouch at her side, but the bird was too quick. Flying at her face, he aimed his claws at her eyes. Instinctively, Vivienne slapped her hands to her face to protect herself, and in that one swift movement the dart she had in her hand grazed her cheek. It was only a graze. It barely sliced the first layer of skin, but it was enough for the powerful poison to take effect. She fell instantly to the floor of the tree house and lay there quite still. The crow cawed in victory while, below, a giant saw rasped into action.

The vicious metal blade of the saw gnawed and bit as the pirates sweated at their task. Soon it had sunk through a quarter of the enormous trunk, then half and then a full three-quarters of the ancient tree. Still, that tree refused to fall. The pirates continued, pairs of exhausted men taking turns to work at either ends of the saw. As they worked, they looked up cautiously from time to time into the web of branches above. Every man wondered what had become of Vivienne Small and her arrows.

'Done a runner, is what,' said one of the pirates.

'Not her, not likely,' said another.

'She'll have something up her sleeve. We know that.'

'Heave to, yer blackguards, before she springs a trap.'

'Maybe Baldwin has pecked out her eyes,' someone suggested, and all of the pirates chuckled.

High above them, Vivienne Small lay unconscious as the effects of the tiny scratch from the dart slowly worked their way through her body. Baldwin the crow was sitting on her chest, staring right at her as if he did indeed intend to pick out her eyes and eat them.

'Vivienne Small is dead,' he squawked. 'Vivienne Small is dead.'

If the dart had gone deeper, she might have been unconscious for a whole day and a night. As it was, Vivienne woke as the tree was starting to tilt in final anguish.

'No, crow, Mothwood is dead!' Vivienne yelled as she flung herself up, spread her injured wings painfully and knocked the bird away. She felt the tree quiver beneath her. There was a shriek of splitting wood. The tree and the tree house pitched sidewards as the saw sliced clean through the trunk. Vivienne clung to the railing. The crow flew at her again, claws swiping at her eyes. Then it gave a shrill cry and fled. Vivienne braced herself for the inevitable plunge to the ground but, for one moment, as if in a final embrace, the nearby trees held her tree and her home. It was all the time she needed. Vivienne leapt onto a railing, her leathery wings swelling as they captured the air. Despite the searing pain in her torn wing, she managed to fly the short distance to a nearby walkway. Behind her, the wooden path sheared away as the mighty tree succumbed. Vivienne's ears filled with the scream of splintering branches.

It hit the forest floor with a crescendo that shook the ground for miles around. In the aftermath, there was no sound at all. No birds called nor grasshoppers sang, no crickets chirped nor bees hummed. The forest was utterly silent. And then a great cheer went up from Mothwood's men.

Chapter Nine

The sun was high in the sky by the time Tuesday and Baxterr reached the edge of the Peppermint Forest. They were hot and tired and footsore and hungry, and glad to leave behind the heat of the day and the open grassland for the fragrant shade of the forest. Tuesday would have loved nothing more than to flop down on the ground and rest for a few minutes, but Baxterr whined, his ears flattened. Suddenly the ground beneath their feet trembled and there was a distant rumble. Had it been a roll of thunder—or an earthquake? Tuesday waited but there was nothing more.

Baxterr barked.

'It's okay. We'll be there in no time now,' she said to him. 'If we go straight into the forest, then we'll come to a stream. We follow it downstream until we find the Twining Bridge. We cross that and then follow the golden moss beds until we reach a line of tree ferns that looks rather like a front fence.'

Tuesday was showing off a little, but it was only to her dog, and she was sure that he didn't mind. In the many hours she had spent studying the little maps that were drawn on the inside covers of the hardback editions of all the Vivienne Small adventures, she had never imagined that it would be so useful to have those maps memorised.

Tuesday had never been in a forest before. At home there was City Park, which had plenty of trees, some of which were very big and very old, but it was still nothing like this. Here the trees clustered thickly together, their branches growing high overhead. The light in the forest was almost like twilight, but with a golden-green glow to it. And with every step there was something new to wonder at — a new fern frond uncoiling, a strange leaf pattern, a flower in a shade of blue she'd never seen, the sparkle of a spider's web across the path. There were moss beds growing tiny yellow and white flowers, and on the trunks of the trees were curling fungi with little frilled edges like the lace on a ball gown. At the bottom of the tree trunks were toadstools: some orange, some brown, and even some that were red with large white spots.

As it turned out, the stream *was* easy to find. But the Twining Bridge was quite difficult to cross because of all the branches that stuck out from it, and the fact that the wet trunks that had grown together to make the bridge were as slippery as ice. The golden moss beds too were beautiful but spongy, and walking on them was like walking on damp feather pillows. By the time they reached a glade of towering tree ferns, growing in an orderly row, Tuesday was exhausted from the morning's efforts. And she had noticed something unusual. It was too quiet in the forest. Since they had entered the trees she had heard not a single bird call. Yet she knew the Peppermint Forest rang with birdcalls. This silence made her cautious.

Tuesday knew they would find Vivienne's tree beyond the ferns. Then she would somehow have to get Vivienne's attention—if she was home—and have her throw down the rope ladder she used for visitors. Tuesday's heart was beating fast from the excitement of soon meeting Vivienne Small, and from an increasingly uncomfortable feeling that things were not right.

She pushed her way between the tree ferns and her breath caught in her throat. Bright sunshine was flooding into the forest and the effect was as shocking as if someone had turned on the light in the middle of the night. The gentle gloom of the forest was shattered. Instead of a vast tree reaching so high you'd have to drop your head right back to see the branches soaring into the canopy, and a trunk so wide that you could take a whole minute to walk around it, there was only clear blue sky and the freshly sawn stump of a giant peppermint tree.

She and Baxterr gazed in shock at the massive trunk that had fallen, crushing everything in its path. She understood what Baxterr had been sensing all morning and the cause of the eerie silence that had settled on the forest. Tuesday held back tears. Together she and Baxterr scrambled up and made their way along the length of the fallen trunk, stepping over broken limbs and clearing away smaller branches, surveying the chaos of flattened trees and bushes caught in the fall. At last they came to what had been the upper branches of the tree and there they discovered the wreckage of Vivienne's house. The thatched roof, the oval windows and the arched front door were all in pieces. The wooden ladders and curved verandah railings were familiar to Tuesday, as were the flowering creeper and woven bird-feeders that hung from them. In among the splintered timbers were shards of smashed glass, broken crockery and furniture.

'Vivienne!' Tuesday said. Her heart hammered inside her body again, this time in panic. 'Vivienne! Baxterr, you don't think she … that she might have been here when whoever did this? She might be under here, she might be crushed—Baxterr, we have to find her!'

Tuesday swung into action, pulling away broken branches and lifting shattered walls. Baxterr, his nose quivering, tried to catch a trace of Vivienne's scent. Together they searched, and though they found pieces of Vivienne's life – her leather shoes (very small), her spyglass (broken), and her Lucretian blowpipe (intact but without darts), there was no sign of Vivienne.

When she was quite sure that Vivienne was not buried beneath the wreckage, Tuesday sat down with her head in her hands.

'Perhaps Vivienne wasn't here when it happened,' she said to Baxterr. 'Or maybe she's been captured by … well, by whoever did this. And maybe Mum is with her. Maybe that's what's happened. Maybe they've been captured together. And there's only one person who would do this kind of thing. Mothwood!'

Baxterr continued to forage in the fallen branches as if he were looking for something specific. At last, he looked up and barked excitedly. Tuesday leapt to her feet and dashed over to Baxterr. What he had found was not Vivienne Small. Instead, he was nosing at a glass bottle that was nestled – quite unbroken – under a splintered shelf. Inside the bottle was a miniature sailboat with a gleaming red hull and white sails the size of daisy petals.

'Oh, you good dog!' Tuesday said, as she gazed at the tiny boat in wonder. It was Vivienne Small's boat, *Vivacious*.

'You know, Baxterr, if Vivienne Small and Mum have been captured by Mothwood, then they are almost certainly on *The Silverfish*. Perhaps that's why I saw *The Silverfish* through the binoculars! Because that's where we have to go! To *The Silverfish*. So, of course, we're going to have to set sail too, aren't we?'

'Ruff,' said Baxterr, tipping his head to one side and looking concerned.

'You're right,' said Tuesday, peering into the bottle where the tiny vessel lay. 'It *is* a bit small. What we need, doggo ... what we need is ...'

Tuesday searched about in the crushed leaves until she found a small object, which she held out triumphantly for Baxterr to see. It was a tiny glass marble. One side of it was silver, the other gold.

Chapter Ten

At Brown Street, Serendipity and Denis sat at the kitchen table. Serendipity was finishing off two crumpets with honey and a cup of strong tea. Neither one of them spoke. Having been awake the entire night, Serendipity was deeply tired, and, though he had slept a little, Denis's face was creased and grey. The house felt very empty and very quiet without Tuesday and Baxterr.

Serendipity was thinking about the years she had spent cultivating Tuesday's imagination, and wondering if she had done the right thing. Stories had been more than a bedtime ritual. She had made sure that stories happened at breakfast, lunch and dinner, as well as any time in between. Stories happened while they were cleaning their teeth, or vacuuming the hall, or running in the rain on the way home from the park.

'What about...' Tuesday would say.

'Yes, what about...' Serendipity would reply, and then the two of them would be off, making up a story.

If Serendipity was away on a book tour she didn't send home postcards with *Having a wonderful time, wish you were here* written on them. She sent home postcards with sentences like this:

In China they eat their noodles, and in France they walk their poodles but...

And Tuesday and Denis would write back: *in Australia, I have heard, that they play their didgeridoodles.*

At the dinner table, Denis might suddenly say: 'My brother Michael loved peas.'

Then Serendipity would say: 'He ate them night and day. He stuck them on his bedroom door. He mashed them with a fork and had them on toast for breakfast.'

Then Tuesday would say: 'He lined them up on the edge of the bath.'

'But one day…' Denis would say.

And so the story would go on.

Tuesday's favourite thing at bedtime when she was very small had been to say to Serendipity: 'Tell me a story out of your voice.'

And Serendipity would give her three options.

'Well,' she'd say, 'I can tell you about The Golden Swan, The House with the Blue Gate, or The Carpenter and the Walnut.'

And Tuesday would choose. Then Serendipity would begin with only her imagination to guide her along.

'My mother makes hats for the cats of the Queen of England,' one story began.

Another began: 'If you knew my sister, you'd never want to be me.'

It wasn't that Serendipity hadn't seen it coming. She had seen that a big story would come, so big it would sweep Tuesday off her feet, but she hadn't expected it while Tuesday was still so young. Serendipity realised it was the breadth and depth of her daughter's imagination that worried her most. What might befall her precious Tuesday, who was still just a girl, in a place where stories were not just words?

As if he heard her thoughts, Denis said, 'What happens to a girl who visits your place, the place writers go to, when she's just Tuesday's age?'

'Well,' said Serendipity, 'it will be the most fantastic adventure she's ever had.'

'What sort of world do you think she'll find?' Denis asked.

Serendipity thought of Tuesday, of Tuesday's imagination. And then it came to her. Of course. All in a rush, Serendipity remembered Louella-Bella, Tuesday's best imaginary friend. In her mind she saw a much younger Tuesday, in her red overalls with the yellow pocket, standing beside Louella-Bella. They were at the zoo, eating from either end of a large lime-green earthworm. And yes, Louella-Bella looked just the way Tuesday had always described her, with a cloud of white frizzy hair, and rainbow-coloured tights under a hot-pink pinafore. Serendipity smiled.

'Perhaps she's found Louella-Bella and they're off at the zoo,' she said hopefully.

Denis frowned.

'It strikes me that the young lady I saw flying out the window might have rather grown out of Louella-Bella.'

'Oh?' said Serendipity, looking crestfallen. 'I expect you're right.'

Serendipity tried again, this time with more grown-up thoughts. The world that came to her, in fleeting black and white images, seemed to be a schoolyard. It was something like the high school to which Tuesday would go soon. It had wide courtyards and bench seats under oak trees and old buildings made of stone. The students who clustered together in groups, talking and laughing, were terribly tall and terribly grown up. One of them in particular drew Serendipity's attention—a girl with reddish-blonde hair, a sparkling smile, and a smattering of freckles on a nose that was neither too big nor too small. It was Tuesday a little older than she was now. Serendipity imagined this Tuesday swinging her school bag over one shoulder and crossing the school grounds with two friends.

'Perhaps her story is a mystery. Set in a high

school, where...' Serendipity began, and then trailed off, rubbing at her eyes that were so itchy with sleeplessness.

A weary weight settled upon her shoulders.

'I think you're forgetting that she went looking for *you*...' Denis said.

'So, what do *you* think she's doing? I'm so tired I can't even think.'

'Well,' said Denis, 'I wouldn't be at all surprised if she didn't run into the world of Vivienne Small's adventures.'

'But why?' Serendipity asked, yawning. 'Why would she imagine that?'

'Because that's where she'd expect to find you.'

Serendipity thought for a moment, then turned grey with worry.

'What if she ... oh, no. Oh, Denis – Vivienne's world is full of danger,' she said, her face crumpling. 'Tuesday's not... well, she's never been... she could so easily get hurt... she...'

'Come with me,' said Denis, rising from the table and putting his arms around his wife.

Together they walked up the stairs to their bedroom. Denis folded down the bedcovers and handed Serendipity her pyjamas from the hook on the back of the door.

'Sleep now. I'll wait up and when she arrives home, we'll wake you,' he said. And just as he had done for Tuesday the night before, Denis tucked Serendipity into bed. This time he did turn off the light and close the door, which was just the way Serendipity liked it.

Chapter Eleven

Tuesday and Baxterr emerged on the far side of the Peppermint Forest and found themselves on a cliff overlooking the Restless Sea, which was crumpled by a gentle breeze. Waves rolled in on a rocky shoreline below and several giant white clouds ambled across the sky. Before leaving Vivienne's shattered tree house they had consumed most of the Food For The Road they had taken from the Library's buffet and refilled their water bottles at a nearby stream. As they surveyed the scene before them, taking in the cliff path that sloped downwards to the shore and a sandy cove beyond, Tuesday broke off a piece of the chocolate bar for herself, and offered some cheese and biscuits to Baxterr, who gulped them down happily.

When they arrived on the beach, Tuesday took from her backpack the glass bottle containing the tiny boat, then fished in her pocket for the silver and gold marble. She placed the bottle carefully on the sand, unscrewed the two parts of the marble and screwed the silver half onto the neck of the bottle, and the gold half into the small groove in the bottle's base. Then she sat back and watched. The bottle wriggled a little, as if experiencing a small tremor, and then it split open. The two halves of the bottle fell onto the sand and the boat began to grow. At first it was no bigger than a bath toy, then it was the size of a model you might set upon your shelf. Tuesday and Baxterr watched as it continued growing into a dinghy suitable for one or two sailors at most. It was exactly the same as its tiny model version, with a gleaming red hull and two crisp white sails. These sails caught the breeze and flapped, tugging at the ropes that lay coiled on the deck.

'Well, hello, *Vivacious*!' said Tuesday, very pleased with her work.

She had read about Vivienne Small doing this countless times: taking her yacht-in-a-bottle and her marble out of her pocket, then escaping from Mothwood under sail, outmanoeuvring *The Silverfish* until she had reached safety.

Tuesday ruffled Baxterr's ears and said: 'What do you think of *that*, doggo?'

Baxterr barked his approval.

'We do have a small problem,' said Tuesday. 'Which is that I don't have the first clue how to sail a boat. Still, we have to try. Because I expect that if we set sail, we are almost certain to come across *The Silverfish*. And Vivienne Small and Mum, with any luck.'

Tuesday shivered a little at the thought of encountering *The Silverfish* and Carsten Mothwood. If her mother had been captured by Mothwood, Tuesday hadn't the first idea of how she might rescue her. But she also knew that if Vivienne Small was there, then Vivienne would somehow make the impossible possible.

Tuesday unlaced her shoes and peeled off her socks. She collected the two halves of the glass bottle off the sand and rolled them carefully inside one sock. With an attitude of resolve, she shoved all her belongings into her backpack and stowed them into a little cupboard at the front of the boat. She zipped herself into the orange life jacket that lay in the bottom of the dinghy, then pushed the vessel across the wet sand and into the swirling water.

Vivacious rocked wildly as the first wave caught her, and Tuesday quickly scrambled aboard, but Baxterr was still in the water and barking. She jumped out of the boat again just as another wave hit and this time *Vivacious* was caught side-on. The boat tipped onto its side, sails dragging in the water, ropes streaming overboard. Tuesday battled to haul the boat upright, but it wasn't easy. She succeeded with some effort, while Baxterr barked.

'Quiet, doggo,' Tuesday said sharply, and Baxterr hushed.

Tuesday pulled the bow of the boat back into the waves.

'In,' she said to Baxterr, 'and sit down.'

Tuesday was learning the first rule of skippering a boat: that it is necessary at times to be a little bossy with your crew. Tuesday walked the boat out deeper this time, water rising up around her knees. She held on grimly as the first wave tried to tip the boat up. She checked the sails and then tightened a couple of ropes. Instantly the sails filled with wind and the little boat leapt out of Tuesday's grasp. Baxterr, aboard alone, looked back at her just before the next wave caught *Vivacious*, again tipping her sidewards, sending Baxterr sprawling into the sea. He bobbed up quickly and swam ashore. Tuesday heaved the boat out of the shallows, righting it on the shore once more, but both girl and dog were entirely bedraggled.

Tuesday slumped. She sat on the sand and unzipped the life jacket that felt quite tight around her middle. Baxterr stood beside her and – as if to remind her that it had been her bright idea for him to sit in the boat in the first place – shook himself vigorously all over her.

'I'm sorry, doggo,' she said. 'Are you all right?'

Baxterr gave a small whine as if to reassure her that it was only his pride that was hurt.

'Oh, Baxterr, what are we going to do? I don't know *anything* about sailing.'

Baxterr lay in the sand and rolled onto his back. He seemed very happy to be on dry land. And while Tuesday felt much the same, she kept looking at the boat and at the sea as if they were a puzzle she simply had to solve. It was a long way back to the Library to ask for help, and even if she went there, the Librarian was unlikely to be particularly happy with Tuesday; not after she had dashed off into the world of Vivienne Small against the Librarian's best advice.

'But I'm utterly stuck,' Tuesday thought. 'And the Librarian is the only one who can help me.' She thought again of the Library with its endless bookshelves, the binoculars on the balcony and the writers at work at their desks. The great word *Imagine* carved above the doors. But how did imagining help in a situation like this? she wondered.

'I'm just going to have to work it out,' Tuesday said. She clambered into the little dinghy as it sat on the shore. The sails were flapping and the wooden beam that held the large sail to the mast swung towards her. She pushed it away, but it jerked back, the boat tilting wildly. Ducking to avoid being hit in the head, Tuesday fell out of the boat, and landed face down on the beach.

She rolled over and spat sand out of her mouth. She needed water. And not salt water. She dusted herself off and reached into the boat where she had stowed her backpack. As she was rummaging around for her water bottle she spotted something wrapped in an old oilcloth and bound tightly with a length of twine. She rinsed the sand from between her teeth, took a few swallows of water and replaced the lid.

Pulling the oilcloth parcel onto her lap, she worked at the string. The knot slipped easily. Layer after layer, she unbound the parcel, until inside she found a book. It had a photograph of a small dinghy on the cover and it was titled *How to Sail Small Boats: A Beginner's Guide*, by S.W. Luffy. Within its covers were pictures, photographs and diagrams. There were simple instructions and explanations on such topics as *Knowing Your Sailing Terms*, *Rigging Your Small Boat*, *Launching Your Small Boat*, *Reading the Wind*, *Knowing your Sails*, *Trimming Your Sails*, and *Sailing to a Destination*.

Tuesday read swiftly and carefully, quickly

gaining an understanding of how, when launching *Vivacious*, she must head the bow of the boat into the wind so as not to be knocked over by waves. How she must go aboard from the stern, so as not to tip the boat. She must insert the centreboard (a large slice of varnished wood she had seen on the floor of *Vivacious*, not knowing its purpose) into the slot in the middle of the boat to ensure it sailed in the right direction, but only when the water was deep enough. She also had to steer with a 'rudder' attached to the handle at the back of the boat called 'the tiller'–rather like steering a car, she presumed, except that the sea was the road and the tiller was her steering wheel. Ropes were called 'sheets' and the wooden beam that had almost knocked her senseless was called 'the boom'.

Tuesday scanned the horizon. Though she saw no sign of Mothwood's ship, she did notice the sun was no longer high in the sky, though the day was still warm. She felt sure she would have a better view once they had sailed out beyond the cove.

'We'd best make some progress before nightfall,' she said.

Calling Baxterr to her, Tuesday zipped her life jacket once again and set about preparing for another launch. She commanded a reluctant Baxterr aboard before pulling the bow of the boat out as far as she could beyond the breaking point of the waves. Water rose up around her waist. Baxterr watched her warily from inside the boat. Next she slipped along the boat, all the while holding onto the sides, and lowered the rudder into the water, then she kicked herself in over the stern. She quickly pushed the centreboard into the slot and, holding fast to the tiller, she headed *Vivacious* away from the wind, pulling the ropes—no, *sheets*, she reminded herself—to tighten the sails.

And then, by a beautiful miracle of wind and wood and water, they were sailing. Gulls on a rock observed the small craft silently and Tuesday couldn't help but feel rather delighted as she passed by them. Here she was, at sea, and looking for all the world like a sailor. Though he would normally have barked at the birds, Baxterr ignored them, pointing his nose straight ahead as if he understood that to be a sea dog was a noble thing.

They sailed away from the beach and past the

rocky point. A long stretch of coast led away south. Tuesday was determined to follow the cliffs, but she realised that if she was not careful, the breeze would take her in the opposite direction, out to the open sea. She would have to do what the book had termed 'tacking'. She pulled the book out once more, furiously reading that part again. It seemed easy enough. But of course it wasn't easy at all.

Away from the protection of the bay, the breeze had stiffened. Small white-capped waves were running across the sea and *Vivacious* had picked up speed. As soon as Tuesday pushed the tiller firmly to one side to change direction, the sails flapped and banged loudly above her and the boat jolted. Baxterr barked. The boom swung wildly again, making Tuesday dive to the floor. Tuesday glimpsed the direction she wanted to go and pulled on the tiller while grasping at the sheets to bring in the sails. The little boat steadied and they were underway again, this time towards the cliffs in the distance. Tuesday's heart slowed to a normal pace. Baxterr looked at her as if he were wondering what was in store next.

'It's all right, doggo,' she said gently, breathing out. 'We're okay now.'

She looked ahead and saw the sea darkening.

'What's that on the water?' she said.

A dark line on the water ahead means only one thing to a sailor. Wind. When it reached them, it buffeted *Vivacious*. The sails filled and the boat tipped precariously. Tuesday leaned back over the side of the boat, holding fast to the tiller. The boat flattened a little and they flew across the water, spray from the oncoming waves washing over the bow of the boat and drenching Tuesday. She tasted salt on her lips and blinked it from her eyes. The boat continued across the water, the breeze strengthening. The cliffs ahead were coming up fast and Tuesday could see she would soon have to change direction again. She was heading for a crop of rocky islands. Gulls circled in the sky. Tuesday could see thick brown strands of kelp clinging to the rocks ahead, washing into the water as the breaking waves receded.

She steeled herself, running through all that she was going to have to do. Her eyes flew from the sails to the water ahead.

'Baxterr, stay there and don't move, no matter what!' she said.

Baxterr whined and hunkered down on the floor. Tuesday pushed the tiller over and tried to release the sails, but the wind was too strong. The sails back-filled and the boat tipped violently. Before they had a moment to think, Tuesday and Baxterr were tumbled into the sea. Instinctively Tuesday kicked away from the boat, turning to watch as *Vivacious* rolled right over, white sails and mast disappearing beneath the sea, leaving nothing but an upturned hull washing towards the rocks. Tuesday swam around the boat, calling to Baxterr.

But Baxterr did not reply.

Chapter Twelve

'Baxterr!' Tuesday called again.

She dived under the water. Below in the clear green of the sea she could make out the mast pointing towards the sea floor and the sails billowing gently in the gloom. She came up for air and still Baxterr was nowhere to be seen. She dived again, this time going under the boat and coming up in the space beneath the curve of the floorboards. Here there was air to breathe though the sea was slopping at her neck. She felt frantically about on the submerged deck and as she did so, she brushed against something. Her fingers grasped fur. It was Baxterr! She tried to haul him up, but he was caught. Ropes were twisted around his neck, trapping him underwater. Tuesday forced her fingers under the ropes and began peeling them over Baxterr's head, freeing his legs. Water splashed in her mouth, making her cough. Despite the choking water, she kept at it, working hard until at last Baxterr was free. She hauled him up beside her, but Baxterr's eyes were closed and he was heavy in the water.

'No! No!' she cried, her words echoing in the tiny space under the boat.

Holding Baxterr tight, Tuesday dived from under the boat out to the open sea beyond. As she surfaced she realised that it was only her life jacket keeping them both afloat. She was tired and cold and Baxterr was a dead weight in her arms.

Suddenly, out of the corner of her eye, Tuesday saw something dark leaping along the rocks from the shore. Not something–some*one*. Tuesday wiped salt water from her eyes and blinked. Above the wind, Tuesday could hear yelling.

In one fleet movement the someone leapt from the rocks onto the upturned hull of *Vivacious*, landing as nimbly as a gymnast.

'What on earth do you think you're doing? You can't bring her in like that!' yelled the small girl.

'My dog has drowned!' Tuesday called. 'Help!'

The girl noticed Baxterr in Tuesday's arms and she nodded.

'Hold his head up,' she yelled over the wind. 'Swim for the shore!'

Then the girl dived beneath the boat. A few moments later *Vivacious* was righted, looking dishevelled, but awaiting instruction. Soon she was underway again and, expertly, the girl sailed the small dinghy the short distance to the shore. Tuesday staggered out of the waves with Baxterr utterly limp in her arms. In a moment the girl was beside her, helping her carry Baxterr up the grey pebbled beach. Together the two girls laid him down on his side.

'Oh!' said the girl in a hushed voice. 'It's a ... no, he can't be a ...'

'He got a rope caught around him and was trapped under the boat when it capsized. Oh please, what we can do? Please, if there's anything ...' Tuesday's words rushed out of her, tears running hot and fast down her cheeks as she looked at Baxterr's lifeless body.

'We must save him,' the girl said with fierce determination, and she ran her hands over Baxterr's sodden fur, feeling his belly, his lungs, his throat, his back.

How different Baxterr looked. He was so silent and still. Tuesday lifted his head onto her lap.

'Oh, doggo, please don't die,' she said.

'You must call him back to you,' the girl said. 'With his real, true name. Tell him he must come back to you.'

'Baxterr,' said Tuesday. 'His name is Baxterr, with a double r.'

The girl lifted one of Baxterr's ears and indicated to Tuesday. And so Tuesday whispered into his ear, 'Baxterr...Baxterr. Come back. Come back to me.'

Baxterr shuddered. He trembled and then a wave of seawater erupted from his mouth and washed over the pebbles. He whined. Another great wave of water escaped him and he whined again.

'There! There you are,' said the small girl with

infinite tenderness, stroking his neck. Baxterr shivered, but his eyes opened and fixed on Tuesday. He gave her a small, reassuring *ruff* and closed his eyes again as if it had taken all his strength to come back from wherever he had been.

'We saved him!' Tuesday said, kissing him on his cheek.

'Where did you find him?' asked the girl.

'Find him?' asked Tuesday, gazing at Baxterr. 'My mother brought him home when I was five.'

The girl said, 'I never thought to see another.'

'A dog?' Tuesday asked, confused.

'A Winged Dog,' the girl said, still patting Baxterr's head as he panted slightly. 'I mean, he's tiny for a Winged Dog, but I'd recognise one anywhere.'

Tuesday had read about Winged Dogs, of course. In the second Vivienne Small book, *Vivienne Small and the Remarkable Return*, the legendary dogs of the Winged Mountains – dogs that were bigger than horses – had fought alongside Vivienne Small and the sea-people of Xunchilla in a fierce battle against an army commanded by Carsten Mothwood. So Tuesday knew that Baxterr was quite clearly not a Winged Dog. Winged Dogs were colossal, to begin with. And then there was the small matter of their having wings.

'It's been a great many years now since the Winged Dogs disappeared,' the girl continued, stroking Baxterr's fur. 'They took to the air and were gone, and though it is said that they flew to another world, nobody knows for certain where it is that they went.'

'Sometimes I pretend that he has wings, you know, but he's not really a Winged Dog,' Tuesday said gently, not wanting to argue with their rescuer.

'Oh, yes he is,' the girl said, and then she delved her hands deep into Baxterr's wet fur and, with great care, spread out before Tuesday a vast, sodden, furry wing.

'No!' Tuesday said.

Baxterr was too exhausted to do more than lift his head a little and grin at Tuesday. But grin he did. She put her arms around him and hugged him.

'Oh, Baxterr,' she exclaimed, tears of relief running down her cheeks. 'You're alive and you've ... you've grown wings!'

'But in future,' said the girl to Tuesday, rather sternly, 'you might want to be a little more careful about how loudly you say his name.'

'His name?' asked Tuesday. 'I don't understand.'

'Don't you know that if the wrong person learned his name then you could lose him forever? It's part of a Winged Dog's magic. Their name is like a key, and you have to keep it safe.'

'But at home, he's not a magical dog,' said Tuesday. 'I mean he definitely doesn't have wings at home. I'd have noticed. We all would have noticed. But he's alive!' she continued. 'And that's all that matters.'

'Home? You're not from here?' asked the girl.

'No,' said Tuesday, 'I just arrived today.'

'And stole my boat,' the girl said.

'*Your* boat?' Tuesday asked.

'Yes!' said the girl. 'My boat.'

And for the first time since coming ashore, Tuesday took her eyes off Baxterr and stared at the girl in front of her. She had dark wavy hair threaded with bright wet feathers, and leather clothes that were wet too. Her gleaming grey-green eyes were looking right back at Tuesday.

Tuesday burst into an excited grin.

'Vivienne – oh my goodness! I'm so sorry. I was so worried about Baxterr that I didn't think, but it's you! *It's you!* Vivienne Small! It's really you!'

Chapter Thirteen

'Yes,' said the girl in surprise. 'I'm Vivienne Small. But who are you?'

'I'm Tuesday,' Tuesday said, realising she had no idea how to proceed. 'Tuesday McGillycuddy.'

And here she stopped. Although she knew almost everything there was to know about Vivienne Small, it occurred to her that Vivienne Small knew nothing whatsoever about *her*. Baxterr whined. With some effort he scrambled to his feet and shook himself. In a majestic action – as if he always did this – he stretched out two marvellous shaggy brown wings. Then he gave a yelp of pain.

Vivienne jumped to her feet and examined his wings.

'I think he's been cut while trying to get free from the boat. Well, you and me both, Baxterr,' she said. Turning her back, Vivienne spread her own blue wings to show Tuesday a deep tear on the right side.

'It happened yesterday,' said Vivienne, 'so no flying for me just now. And none for this boy either. Wings heal quite fast, though. I wouldn't be at all surprised if he can fly again in a day or two. You're very lucky, you know. There would be people who would kill to have him for their own.'

Tuesday's head was spinning. Was Baxterr really a Winged Dog? She thought back to the day he had arrived at Brown Street when he was just a tiny golden-brown puppy. Serendipity had come down the stairs from her writing room with a little dog in her arms. Even Denis had looked surprised, though he had quickly recovered his equilibrium and popped out to the supermarket to buy puppy food and all the other things a small, unexpected dog might need. All those years ago, her mother had said to her: 'Tuesday, this is your very own dog, and because he's your very own dog, you and only you must name him.'

'Baxter*r*,' Tuesday had said, knowing instantly that this was his name.

'Baxter*rrr*?' her mother had said. 'Why Baxter*rrr*?'

'Because *rrr* is what he will say if anyone ever tries to hurt me.'

And so Baxterr – with a double r – he was. But had her mother brought him home from another world, from this world of Vivienne Small where Winged Dogs grew to be bigger than horses, the fiercest of protectors? Tuesday could only sit and wonder at how such a thing had happened. Was Baxterr truly one of the last Winged Dogs?

Sitting between Vivienne and Tuesday, Baxterr sneezed. And in a strange moment of synchronicity so did both Tuesday and Vivienne. Not once, not twice, but three times the two girls and the dog sneezed in perfect unison. And maybe it was the surprise of meeting one another or the relief of Baxterr being alive, or just the fact of having shared a bout of sneezing, but the two girls began laughing and then they found they couldn't stop. And whenever they did pause for a moment, Baxterr sneezed again and they started over until their stomachs hurt from laughing. By the time the sneezing was finally over, and the girls had wiped their eyes, they were friends.

'I think we'd better get dry,' Vivienne said. She pointed high up in the cliff behind them. 'I have a cave up there.'

Together the two girls pulled *Vivacious* up the shore and tied her to a tree growing out of the cliff face.

'How did you know about *Vivacious*?' Vivienne asked Tuesday.

'That she was more than just a model boat, you mean? That she could be made bigger?' Tuesday asked.

'Yes. How could you *possibly* have known about *that*?'

'Oh, it was just luck, I guess,' Tuesday said. 'Baxterr found her and then I found the marble and ...' She looked up at Vivienne, who was clearly impressed, and then, not wanting to be untruthful, she added, 'I did once read about something like that in a book.'

'Really?' Vivienne said, looking very intrigued.

'Oh,' said Tuesday, rushing to change the subject, 'you'd better have these back.'

She fetched her backpack, which was still tucked inside the cupboard on the boat, and fished out the two halves of the glass bottle from which *Vivacious* had so magically emerged. Vivienne took them from her gratefully.

Then she said solemnly, 'So you saw the tree house?'

'Yes,' said Tuesday. 'I'm so sorry.'

'But what were you doing there?'

'Looking for you,' said Tuesday.

'You were?' asked Vivienne perplexedly, as she continued furling the sails around the mast of *Vivacious*.

'Yes. I thought you might help me find my mother. You see, that's why I'm here. She's lost and...'

'Your mother?' asked Vivienne.

'Yes, my mother's name is Serendipity Smith,' said Tuesday hesitantly, realising that this was the very first time in her life that she had said these words.

Tuesday watched Vivienne's reaction carefully, and it seemed to Tuesday that even though Vivienne's lips were almost blue with cold, her cheeks flushed a little at the mention of Serendipity's name. Did the characters of books know their authors' names? Surely they did. But, then, maybe they didn't.

'She's about this tall,' said Tuesday, indicating a little way above her own head. 'And she has short brown hair. Or maybe she is this tall' – Tuesday reached high above her head – 'and has long red hair. It depends. She might be wearing a beautiful velvet coat, and knee-high boots. Or she might just be wearing jeans and a black top. Either way, though, she's likely to have a pencil behind her ear. Have you seen her?'

'Did you say "Serendipity"?' Vivienne asked.

'Yes,' said Tuesday, holding her breath.

'I think I might...' Vivienne started, looked embarrassed, and then stopped and eyed Tuesday warily. 'No, no. It's not possible. The person I'm thinking of... well, even if her name *was* Serendipity, she couldn't possibly be your mother.'

'Why not?'

'Just not, you know,' said Vivienne, in an evasive way. And then, shrugging, she said: 'I'm very cold. Aren't you?'

Tuesday was desperate to see what else Vivienne knew, but she was also bitterly cold. She would have liked a cup of hot chocolate and some toast with marmalade.

'Let's go and make some toast, and maybe a hot chocolate?' suggested Vivienne, as if she had read Tuesday's mind.

'Okay,' said Tuesday, rather in awe. 'But aren't you going to put *Vivacious* back in her bottle?'

Vivienne, who had already begun scrambling up the cliff, turned and looked out to sea, scanning the horizon.

'Not just yet,' she said. 'We might need to make a quick getaway. Mothwood's men will still be on the lookout for me, I imagine. C'mon, doggo,' she added to Baxterr, who followed her up the narrow path that was well hidden by boulders and small bushes.

'Doggo,' remarked Tuesday to the girl ahead. 'That's funny. That's what I call him.'

But Vivienne didn't appear to hear her.

Some time later, beside Vivienne's campfire, Tuesday sat wiping her bowl clean with a chunk of bread. Her cheeks glowed in the heat and she lifted her head from time to time to watch the smoke disappear up through a hole in the roof of the cave. Tuesday's backpack and clothes were hung on the line to dry beside Vivienne's breeches and shirt. Baxterr lay at the mouth of the cave surveying the coming night. His fur was dry again and his wings were folded at his side, the injured one carefully doctored with a special ointment that Vivienne had provided. His stomach was filled with the food that Vivienne had given him from a pot by the campfire. All three were entirely full, having consumed a wonderful backward meal that began with hot chocolate and marmalade toast and ended with potatoes in their jackets and a delicious, fragrant stew.

The cave above the sea was fitted out with a small bed, a chair, a table, one shelf of cooking equipment and another of small treasures. As the girls had prepared the food, Vivienne had explained the significance of each item on the shelf of treasures, including several beautiful shells, two long black spirals of dried seaweed, a compass and a large brass ship's bell that Tuesday knew Vivienne had once stolen from *The Silverfish*. She let Vivienne recount the story, enjoying it anew. Though she'd read the story plenty of times, in the pages of *Vivienne Small and the River of Rythwyck*, it was very special to hear the tale told by Vivienne herself.

Both Tuesday and Vivienne were wrapped in blankets. The fire had been roused to a merry, crackling blaze. The breeze had settled, as breezes often do at nightfall, and the sea below them was as dark and smooth and shiny as the skin of an aubergine.

'Tell me where you're from,' said Vivienne, as she put her own plate aside and watched the fire between them.

'Well,' said Tuesday, 'it's sort of like here – but different.'

'What sort of adventures do you have?'

'No real ones,' confessed Tuesday. 'This is the biggest adventure I've ever had.'

'Today?' asked Vivienne.

'Yes, actually,' said Tuesday. It seemed remarkable to Tuesday that she had only arrived this morning.

'Then what happens to you on other days?' Vivienne asked.

'I go to school,' said Tuesday.

'School?'

'Yes, you know, where we learn to read and write. And do maths.'

'Maths,' said Vivienne as if she was trying out the word for the first time.

'Yes,' said Tuesday. 'And Baxterr meets me every day after school and he pulls me along on my rollershoes, which are these shoes with wheels in the heels so that you can roll along the ground.'

Vivienne's eyes widened. 'They sound excellent!' she said.

'They are,' Tuesday agreed.

She stretched her bare feet nearer the fire.

'What's your house like? Is it a tree house?' Vivienne asked.

'No,' said Tuesday, sounding a little disappointed. 'Just an ordinary house. It's tall and narrow, with five storeys.'

'It has five storeys?' Vivienne asked curiously.

162

'Yes,' said Tuesday. 'We've lived there since I was born. I've never lived anywhere else.'

'Who do you live with?'

'I don't have any brothers or sisters,' said Tuesday, 'so I just live with my mum and dad.'

Having said this, Tuesday sat bolt upright. Meeting Vivienne had been so remarkable and wonderful that Tuesday had almost entirely forgotten what she was here for. Outside, it was well after nightfall and she still had no idea of how she was ever going to find Serendipity or be back for breakfast.

'What's the matter?' Vivienne asked, also sitting upright and listening keenly. Baxterr stirred and looked back at them both.

'It's my mother,' said Tuesday. 'I was having such a lovely time that I forgot for a little while about finding her.'

'Oh yes,' said Vivienne. 'Your mother. What's her name again?'

'Serendipity.'

'Serendipity,' Vivienne repeated quietly. 'Is that her real name?'

'Well, she was christened Sarah, and some

163

people call her that, but out of the two names I'd say Serendipity is who she truly is.'

'And you thought I could help you to find her,' mused Vivienne.

'Yes,' said Tuesday.

Vivienne looked deeply thoughtful for a moment.

'Tuesday,' she said at last, 'have you ever known anyone who wasn't exactly real? Someone maybe only you could see?'

'Yes,' said Tuesday. 'I had a friend like that. Her name was Louella-Bella. I used to drive Mum and Dad mad by making them set her a place at the table, and do up her seatbelt in the car, and tuck her in and kiss her goodnight. She even had a toothbrush of her own for a while.'

'An *imaginary* friend,' Vivienne said.

'Yes,' said Tuesday.

'Well, I seem to remember someone called Serendipity. Someone who might be a kind of imaginary friend. To me. Yes, she's been here,' said Vivienne very carefully, as if she was saying something private.

'Do you know where she is now?' Tuesday asked eagerly.

'No. She comes when she comes and she goes when she goes.'

'When was the last time you think you saw her?' Tuesday asked.

'I can't remember,' said Vivienne. 'It might have been yesterday, or ages ago. It's like a dream that seems vivid while you're having it, but that you can hardly remember once you wake up.'

'Well, if she's not here with you, then the only idea I have is that I think she's somewhere near The End,' Tuesday said. 'Would you be able to take me there, do you think?'

'The End?' said Vivienne. She looked puzzled. 'I'd be happy to help you, but I've never heard of it.'

'Are you sure?' asked Tuesday. 'I would have thought you'd know everywhere there is to know here.'

'Well, usually I do, but I don't know The End. What does it look like?'

'I'm not sure,' said Tuesday simply. 'But whatever it looks like, I think Mothwood might be there too. In fact, I thought Mothwood must have captured my mother.'

'Mothwood?' said Vivienne Small. 'Mothwood's at The End all right! He's stone cold dead.'

'Mothwood? Dead?' Tuesday gasped. 'Really? But how?'

'Oh, let's say he had a little fall,' Vivienne said, her eyes twinkling. 'Off the Cliffs of Cartavia. That's why his men destroyed my home. It was their revenge.'

'Because you killed Mothwood? You mean to say that you *really, finally, absolutely* killed Mothwood?'

Tuesday felt overawed at this news. She supposed it made sense that Vivienne Small would kill Carsten Mothwood at the end of a book called *Vivienne Small and the Final Battle*, but to hear it from Vivienne Small herself was remarkable.

'Aren't you pleased?' Vivienne asked. She didn't seem the least bit surprised that Tuesday knew who Mothwood was.

'Yes!' said Tuesday. 'I mean it's fantastic. But somehow it's also a little strange.'

The two girls paused, and on either side of the fire, each gave an identical shrug and a sigh.

'Yes,' they agreed in unison.

In their hearts they both knew, even though Mothwood had been a terrible villain, life wouldn't be the same without him.

'Mothwood would know where The End is,' said Vivienne, her face lighting up. 'He has the best maps in all the world.'

'Yes,' Tuesday said, frowning. 'But he's dead.'

'So he won't be needing his maps anymore. We could go and get them,' continued Vivienne. 'From *The Silverfish*.'

'Now?' asked Tuesday, slightly alarmed.

'We'll sleep for a few hours first,' Vivienne said. 'It's best to tackle adventure when you're well rested.'

Vivienne made up an extra bed beside the fire, piling rough blankets on the sandy floor of the cave. Then she took her own mattress and blankets from her small bed and put them on the other side of the fire.

'You have the mattress,' said Vivienne.

'Oh, I couldn't,' said Tuesday.

'I insist,' said Vivienne courteously. 'You're my guest.'

'Well, thank you,' said Tuesday, who knew that the best thing to do when people were very generous was to accept their offerings graciously.

Tuesday lay down on the mattress and arranged her blankets, and as soon as she had done so, Baxterr came to the side of her bed and put up a paw by way of asking permission to climb in with her.

'Do you mind if he sleeps here?' Tuesday asked Vivienne.

'Not a bit,' Vivienne said, as she curled up in her own bed.

Tuesday closed her eyes, thought for a moment, and then opened them again.

'Vivienne,' said Tuesday, 'you haven't said anything about *your* mother and father. Not a word.'

Tuesday knew there was no mention of Vivienne's family, anywhere, in any of the first four Vivienne Small books. She had often asked her mother, but Serendipity just shrugged and said it wasn't part of the story.

'Oh, I never had any parents,' said Vivienne carelessly.

'But of course you did,' said Tuesday. 'How else did you get born?'

'I came out of an egg,' said Vivienne.

'No, you didn't. You couldn't have,' said Tuesday, laughing.

'I did,' said Vivienne. 'It's true.'

'But then you wouldn't have a belly button,' said Tuesday thoughtfully.

'A what?' Vivienne asked.

Tuesday threw back her blankets and showed Vivienne her belly button. Vivienne gaped.

'I don't have one of those,' she said, pulling down her own blankets.

And sure enough, she didn't. Where everyone else has a belly button, Vivienne Small's belly was as smooth as, well, an egg.

'Hah! Imagine that! But you must have had a mother to lay the egg,' Tuesday contemplated. 'Don't you think? I mean how else was there an egg?'

Vivienne shrugged.

'Maybe there was a mother. But I don't think so, somehow. I think I was just an egg.'

'You could have been dropped from the sky by something,' Tuesday suggested. 'And landed on something soft.'

'I suppose that's possible,' said Vivienne. 'But I'm here and that's all that matters.'

Tuesday snuggled back down under her covers and smiled. She knew some things that no other reader of the Vivienne Small books knew. Vivienne Small had come out of an egg. She had no belly button. And she had an imaginary friend called Serendipity.

'Tell me more about where you live,' Vivienne said, yawning. Tuesday told Vivienne about the people who lived in her street and the teacher she'd had this year at school and the kids she played with and what she liked to do on the weekend. She told her about trying to learn the piano, about her fear that she'd need braces when she got older and she even told Vivienne how she still slept with a small blue bear called Toby who had been her friend since she was very small. Just as Vivienne's life had been so fascinating to Tuesday when she had read about it in the books Serendipity had written, Tuesday's life was very interesting to Vivienne.

Gradually, both girls began to drowse. Tuesday was exhausted in a way that you can only be when you've spent an entire day out of doors and some of it in the sea.

'I don't think I can keep my eyes open a minute longer,' said Tuesday.

'Me neither,' said Vivienne.

'Goodnight, Vivienne Small,' said Tuesday.

'Goodnight, Tuesday McGillycuddy,' said Vivienne.

With Baxterr beside her, she fell into a sleep that was deep and dreamless. Outside, the moon passed across the sky, night birds came and went from their nests in the cliff face and the orange light of the fire sent leaping shapes across the cave walls.

Chapter Fourteen

Though Tuesday's sleep was dreamless, in the tall brown house on Brown Street, Serendipity Smith tossed and turned as though fighting a duel in her sleep. In her dreams she was on a ship in a wild storm. Not any ship, but the hulking, steel giant, *The Silverfish*. Lightning broke over the ship's bow and Mothwood was at the wheel, driving the ship into bigger and bigger seas. On the deck Tuesday appeared and disappeared and each time Serendipity reached for her, Tuesday slipped from her grasp or vanished.

'Tuesday! Tuesday!' Serendipity called out,

her voice scarcely registering above the howling winds and churning water.

Serendipity's dream refocused. *The Silverfish* rested, at anchor, in the eerie light of the pre-dawn. Mothwood's men were gathered on the deck. Lanterns hung from above, illuminating something lying on a table. It was the dead body of Carsten Mothwood. The men had laid him out for his burial at sea. At the first light of dawn, the body would be thrown into the water, but first it must be stitched into a burial shroud.

Serendipity sat up in her bed, eyes wide open, her pulse racing.

'I've got it! I've got it!' she said to herself. 'I know what to do! I know how to reach Tuesday.'

Vivienne bent down and whispered into the ear of the sleeping Tuesday.

'Psst,' she said, and when Tuesday opened her eyes she found herself looking right into Vivienne Small's excited face.

Tuesday blinked and yawned.

'What time is it?' she asked.

'Adventure time!' said Vivienne.

The two girls dressed in the dim light, slipping into clothes stiff and warm from drying by the fire, and Vivienne packed a few provisions. Then they were scrambling down the path to the shore, Vivienne leading the way with a small lantern and Baxterr staying close at Tuesday's side, alert for noises in the darkness. Together the girls pulled *Vivacious* from her place above the tide-line and slid her into an inky sea. Each wave in the moonlight brought bright swirls of phosphorescence about the girls' bare feet.

Vivienne worked quickly, unfurling sails and securing ropes. Once *Vivacious* was afloat, Baxterr made a beautiful leap into the boat, clearly unperturbed by the events of the day before. Tuesday scrambled aboard while Vivienne waded deep into the water, steadying the boat as it rode up on an incoming wave. Then, in one seamless movement, she leapt aboard, took the tiller and sailed them away from the shore. Tuesday observed the deftness of the launch, noting the gentle way Vivienne guided *Vivacious*, and she felt unbridled admiration.

The moon lit their way and the sea was a

dark quilt of diamonds. Tuesday realised with a shudder that here she was, on one of Vivienne Small's notorious raids of *The Silverfish*. She felt wildly excited and utterly terrified all at once. She turned back to Vivienne at the tiller.

'Mothwood is definitely dead, isn't he?' she asked.

'Oh yes,' said Vivienne.

'But how did you kill him?'

'I didn't exactly *kill* him,' said Vivienne, but Tuesday could make out her grin in the darkness. 'If he'd shown the tiniest ounce of decency, he wouldn't have died. But he did die. Right there.'

She pointed ahead into the night.

'He fell from the top of the cliffs to the very bottom. He most likely broke every bone in his body.'

Tuesday wanted to know much more, and at the same time, she didn't. It seemed wrong to know too much about the ending of a book she had waited so long to read. So she bit her lip to stop herself asking any questions, ruffled the fur on Baxterr's head and tucked herself up close to him in order to keep out the breeze.

With Vivienne at the helm, *Vivacious* skipped across the sea like a skier on fresh snow. Tuesday could feel the wind on her face and the taste of salt spray that lifted off the water. Stars peeped through the occasional tear in the clouds. Here she was, sailing in darkness with Vivienne Small, to steal the maps of Carsten Mothwood. Then a chill thought occurred to her.

'Vivienne?' asked Tuesday, breaking the silence that had fallen between them. 'Will Mothwood's *body* be there on *The Silverfish*? I mean, what do they do when a pirate dies?'

'They'll bury him at sea at dawn,' said Vivienne.

'You mean today? When the sun comes up?'

'Yes,' said Vivienne.

'So how are we going to steal the maps, if all the pirates are on board?' Tuesday asked.

'Well, that's the fun part, isn't it?' said Vivienne.

The Cliffs of Cartavia were a ghostly grey as *Vivacious* slid past the wall of rock. Tuesday observed the glowing remains of a great fire still smouldering on the shore. Ahead, unmistakable in the cool light of the moon, was a ship at anchor. Tuesday gazed at the distinctive silhouette of *The Silverfish* with its three masts and razor-sharp prow; the fastest and most feared ship on the sea. What Tuesday didn't see immediately was a flag, bearing an eye and a fish skeleton, at half-mast in honour of the passing of the captain. But Vivienne saw it, and it gave her an idea.

'While they're burying Mothwood, let's get ourselves a little souvenir,' she said to Tuesday, indicating ahead. 'Mothwood's flag.'

Tuesday's eyes widened. 'Oh,' she said.

Vivienne swung the dinghy into the breeze and, with hardly a sound, dropped the mainsail. Then, using only the small sail at the bow to guide them, she slipped *Vivacious* alongside *The Silverfish* next to a metal ladder giving access to the deck. Beside *The Silverfish*, *Vivacious* was as tiny as a thimble next to a bucket. Vivienne furled the jib and secured the tiller. A gust of chilly wind gave Tuesday goosebumps. She wrinkled her nose at the foul smell emanating from the hull of the colossal ship.

From somewhere above them, they could hear

the murmuring of voices, and Tuesday had never been more frightened in her life. She felt sick at the thought of her mother being on this awful ship, captive in some dank cell, manacled and hungry, having lived only on scraps for days. She crept close to Vivienne and whispered right into her ear.

'While you're getting the maps, don't forget to check if my mother is here. I have a bad feeling she's being held hostage.'

Vivienne nodded grimly, then began to climb stealthily up the ladder onto the deck. She disappeared from Tuesday's view momentarily, then reappeared, signalling to Tuesday to come up. They both knew the plan: Vivienne would creep into the captain's cabin and steal the maps while Tuesday kept watch. But now it was time to put the plan into action, Tuesday was terrified.

'Stand guard, doggo,' she whispered to Baxterr. '*Vivacious* is our only hope of escape.'

Baxterr cocked his head and then stood quite still, looking as if he would protect *Vivacious* with his life.

'Good boy,' Tuesday whispered and then, her

legs trembling, she too climbed the ladder to the deck. She quickly slipped into the shadows beside Vivienne.

Together they slid along the wall and Vivienne indicated to Tuesday to look. When Tuesday peeked out, what she saw was the corpse of Carsten Mothwood laid out on a large timber chest on the deck, and though it was dressed in the black shirt and trousers and the dark green cloak that were Mothwood's usual garb, there was something about the body that wasn't quite right. All its limbs were crooked. One arm was laid in a direction that should not be possible for an arm. One knee and the foot below were pitched backwards. Mothwood's head was skewed awkwardly to one side.

Lying beside Mothwood, tucked under his arm, was the lifeless figure of Baldwin, the crow that had attacked Vivienne in her tree house. The old bird's act of revenge had taken the last of his strength. After he had seen the tree fall, he had flown back to *The Silverfish*, laid himself at his dead captain's side, and breathed his final breath. The sailors had decided to bury him with his captain.

Tuesday had never seen a dead body before and it made her mouth go dry. Mothwood looked so very dead, so very grey and still. But she realised as she swallowed that she felt much more comfortable seeing Mothwood dead than she would have felt if he'd been alive.

'It's really him,' she whispered, gripping Vivienne's tiny arm.

'And that miserable bird Bald-One,' whispered Vivienne. 'If he wasn't already dead, I'd have a hard time not killing him myself. But it's good to see some of my handiwork,' she said, indicating the pirates sporting bandages. One of them had a hole right through his cheek. 'From yesterday,' said Vivienne, 'at the tree. Now, wait here and if anyone moves to go below decks, make an owl call.'

An owl call? Tuesday wondered as Vivienne slipped away to the rear of the wheelhouse. Tuesday had never attempted an owl call in her life, but it was too late to tell Vivienne. She would just have to manage it, if the time came.

She promised herself that if she got off the ship alive, and safely home again, she would learn such a good owl call that even an owl wouldn't know the difference.

Down on the deck she could hear the pirates arguing. She edged a little closer and listened.

'Gum cheated!' said a rough voice. 'He had that up his sleeve. That wasn't the stick he pulled out. It's a trick!'

'Blast you, Finger, you're a lying worm, on my honour,' came another voice, a slippery, high-pitched voice.

At this all the pirates chuckled. It was a sure sign when a pirate swore on his honour that he was lying through his teeth.

'What say you, Phlegm?'

'I say we'll do it again,' said a deep and menacing voice, presumably belonging to Phlegm. 'All back in the pot.'

The pirates huddled together and Tuesday heard the rattle of sticks as the pirates each put the stick they had drawn back into a tin can.

Then she heard Finger's rough voice say, 'I object! As bosun, I am in charge of all matters pertaining to sails and rigging and as such, the privilege of sewing our late captain in his final blanket should be mine. Besides, no one is handier with needle and thread than me.'

There were a few grunts of agreement, but Gum said, 'Well, as the first mate, I am – with the captain departed for the afterlife – the new captain of this here vessel and in charge of all ceremonies, so it should by all rights be me that does the sewing of the shroud. Isn't that right, Phlegm?'

'I think with the captain dead, all roles and titles are to be freshly agreed,' said Phlegm.

There were jeers. And then a quarrel broke out with all manner of terrible accusations and cries of 'Finger! Phlegm! Gum! Finger! Phlegm! Gum!'

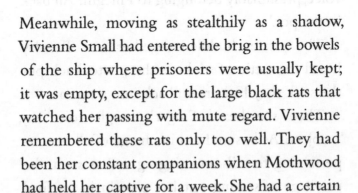

Meanwhile, moving as stealthily as a shadow, Vivienne Small had entered the brig in the bowels of the ship where prisoners were usually kept; it was empty, except for the large black rats that watched her passing with mute regard. Vivienne remembered these rats only too well. They had been her constant companions when Mothwood had held her captive for a week. She had a certain respect for rats, for it had been a rat that had chewed through her ropes and freed her.

Next, Vivienne made her way up through the sailors' quarters and then held her breath as she tiptoed through the stinking, fetid galley where the sailors' meals were prepared. She heard the pirates arguing on the deck above her as she followed the corridor that led to Mothwood's cabin. Once inside, she quietly closed the door and looked about her. In the moonlight spearing through the porthole, she could see that the cabin was quite empty. Clearly no prisoner was held captive here. Silently and carefully, she lit Mothwood's lamp to give herself more light to search by. On the table were charts and a compass, and Vivienne had the eerie impression that Mothwood had stepped from the room just a moment before. To the left was the bed Mothwood had slept in, the sheets untidily crumpled and the pillow bearing a dent where his head had rested only the night before.

'Death is a sudden thing,' Vivienne thought, still amazed by the idea that her enemy was no longer alive.

She picked up a book that lay open on the

bedside table, and was not surprised to find it was a volume of rhyming poetry. That was his way, she thought, to be clever with words.

Once, he had called after her:

> *'If only my words were as sharp as my blade,*
> *In a watery grave, Vivienne Small, you'd be laid.'*

And another time he'd jeered into her face:

> *'If all the world's treasure were offered me,*
> *still your death my greatest joy would be.'*

She shivered, recalling these haunting rhymes, and as she replaced the book on the table, she thought how glad she was never to have to hear Mothwood's voice again.

Up on deck, the argument had come to an abrupt halt. Finger had again drawn the longest straw and this time nobody questioned his right to perform the task. He straightened the captain's twisted limbs and head as best he could, though this was easier said than done.

'He's broken to pieces,' said Liver sorrowfully.

'He is, and no coming back after a fall like that,' muttered Phlegm, and everyone nodded and grunted their agreement.

The sailors launched into a song fit for such an occasion, about the perils of the sea and the beauty of an afterlife beneath the waves. Fixing the canvas tight about the body, they swaddled the captain as well as any newborn baby, with only his bleak face visible in the wrap of canvas. Starting at the feet, Finger began sewing the shroud together while the men held the lanterns high.

The bosun sewed swift and sure, the needle large and sharp, his fingers strong with years of darning sails, mending cloth and plaiting ropes – hence his name, Finger. The rest of the men kept up their singing as the shroud was sewn tight around the corpse.

Below, in Mothwood's cabin, Vivienne heard the song begin. She gathered up the maps off the table. She rolled them tightly and slid them into a long leather cylinder, secured the strap over her shoulder, and retreated. She checked the cabins, port and starboard, as she went. All was dark and still. Tuesday's mother was not here, Vivienne was certain, and there was no evidence she ever had been.

Back on deck, Vivienne slipped down beside Tuesday, who stood transfixed by the sight of the bosun sewing the dead captain into his shroud.

'No prisoners below,' Vivienne whispered.

Tuesday nodded, feeling a mixture of relief and disappointment at this news.

'Got these though,' said Vivienne, taking the map cylinder off her shoulder and laying it down silently on the deck.

Vivienne nudged Tuesday and pointed upwards, where Mothwood's flag fluttered at half-mast.

'Want to come with me?' she whispered, grinning at Tuesday.

'You go,' Tuesday said. 'I'll stand guard.'

This sounded brave, but in truth Tuesday had been struck almost dumb with fear ever since she had arrived on *The Silverfish*. Vivienne, appearing not to notice Tuesday's terror, nodded in agreement. Tuesday watched as her small black shape flitted down the short flight of stairs onto the deck and then across the deck behind the pirates, who were too consumed with the stitching of their captain into his burial shroud to sense that his greatest enemy was just a few feet away.

Chapter Fifteen

Without putting on her dressing gown, or even her slippers, Serendipity Smith bolted out of her bedroom and dashed up the stairs to the writing room where Denis had fallen asleep in the red velvet chair near the open window.

'Denis! Denis!' she said urgently, kneeling beside her husband and shaking him into wakefulness. 'I know. I know how to do it. I know how to get back!'

'What?' asked the befuddled Denis, lifting his head stiffly from where it had fallen, his face marked from the plush pattern of the fabric.

'It's something I'd forgotten. About sailors!' said Serendipity triumphantly.

'What *are* you talking about?'

'When a sailor is buried at sea, the bosun on the ship stitches the body inside a shroud, but there is a tradition that the very last stitch goes right through the sailor's *nose*. You know, the middle bit of your nose, between the nostrils.'

'The septum, Serendipity, my sweet, that super sensitive flesh of the nose is known as the septum,' said Denis, blinking patiently at his wife. 'But please tell me what this has to do with Tuesday. Or anything, for that matter.'

'Well, they do it to make sure the sailor is actually dead, that he's not just unconscious or something. To make sure they're not going to bury anyone alive.'

'I'm not following,' said Denis, perplexed.

'Don't you see? I didn't end the book. Not entirely. *Vivienne Small and the Final Battle* is not over yet, because I didn't put The End at the end. Even though the final battle is over and Mothwood has – apparently – fallen to his death, I didn't finish the book. I decided to sleep on it.

And thank goodness I did, because all I have to do to get back there and find Tuesday is keep the story going. There has to be another chapter!'

'That's all very well, my love, but I fail to see what it has to do with needling noses.'

'Watch me,' she said.

Perching herself on the edge of her chair, Serendipity took from her drawer a new sheet of paper and threaded it into the typewriter.

'Mothwood's not dead. Not dead after all,' she muttered to herself as she readied her hands over the keys and began typing.

Soon she had written about Mothwood's body being laid out on the deck of *The Silverfish*, carried there by his men from the rocks where he had fallen. At nightfall the men returned to the shore and lit a great bonfire on the beach, and there they drank and sang and told stories of the fearless and filthy acts of Carsten Mothwood, now deceased. At some time long after midnight, the men rowed back to *The Silverfish* and gathered together on deck for the ceremony where they would sew the body into the shroud before tossing it overboard into the Restless Sea. From there the body would sink to the sea floor, making food for fish who would surely delight at eating the remains of the great pirate Carsten Mothwood.

As Serendipity wrote, describing how Mothwood's men covered a chest on deck with a salt-stained canvas and lifted the broken form of Mothwood onto it, her words began to lift off the page and circle about her. Serendipity continued, trying not to whoop with glee. Next, she described how the sailors drew straws for who would sew the shroud, for it was an honour of the highest order to do this for a captain, and any sailor worth his salt can sew a seam with a neat and even hand. She wrote about how the pirates cheated and lied and fought over the drawing of straws, and then she stopped, wondering why the words had not scooped her up and floated her out the window. Instead they were hovering in the air above her, not encircling her arms and legs as was usual.

'Denis?' she said quietly, not wanting to frighten the words. 'Something's wrong.'

'There seems to be a shortage of stickiness,' he said. 'A lack of levitation.'

'Why?' Serendipity asked in frustration. 'Why?'

The words hung in the air in silvery loops, just above her head. She reached out as if to catch them, but they slipped from her grasp. She turned back to the typewriter, wielding her fingers like bullets against the keys.

Finger sewed the shroud with perfect stitches while the men watched on, she wrote. *Dawn was approaching. Pirate lore was very specific: a burial must take place at dawn to ensure a quiet resting place for the dead, while a burial at dusk would make a ghost of the dead sailor forever. As dawn approached, Finger sped up the sewing and the pirates held the lanterns high so the light of twenty flames illuminated the corpse.*

The final stitch was imminent and all the sailors held their breath as Finger took the great silver needle, slender and sharp as a blade, and grinned at the men about him. With one strong, sure stroke, Finger grasped both the fabric and the flesh beneath it, plunging the needle through the cloth and into the septum of Mothwood's nose. Before Finger could draw the needle through, a terrible wail erupted from the shroud — a blood-curdling scream of anguish and pain.

These words rose up to join the others. They were shimmering between Serendipity and

Denis, sparkling and drifting. Serendipity stood up from her chair and stepped into them, hoping this would remind the words to wrap themselves around her, but they dispersed and scattered before re-forming near the ceiling. Then, in one single, long thread, they swooped around the room before diving out the open window.

'No!' Serendipity called. 'No!'

She lunged after the end of the silvery tail but the thread slipped through her fingers as if it was satin. It flew away into the inky depths of the sky.

'Denis!' cried Serendipity, her face stricken. 'Denis, Denis, Denis.'

But Denis could do no more than simply peer at the thread vanishing from view.

'I think I might have made things much, much worse,' Serendipity gasped. 'Oh, poor Tuesday. Oh, what have I done?'

On the deck of *The Silverfish*, the singing continued. Tuesday peered up the mast and could just make out a black shape climbing below the flag. Then she saw the dark square of flag disappear, replaced by starry sky. The faintest noise of a jingling reached her as Vivienne unscrewed the cleats holding the flag to the mast.

The pirates' singing ended on a low, mournful note. Finger cut a length of twine and held aloft a huge, curving needle. As he threaded the twine through the eye of the needle, Tuesday saw something unusual. A long filament of glimmering silver drifted through the darkness and wove itself into Finger's thread. The pirates, however, did not appear to have noticed. Every man on deck held his breath as they realised the significance of the moment they were about to witness. Finger gripped the canvas and within it the nose of Carsten Mothwood. With a dramatic flourish he lifted the needle high into the air and then plunged the final stitch into the septum of Mothwood's nose.

There was a blood-curdling screech loud enough to shake the stars in the heavens. Nobody moved. All were struck dumb. The corpse of Mothwood wriggled and writhed, the needle still protruding from the nose. A muffled voice inside the shroud shrieked: 'Aaaggghhh! Get me out of here. Get this thing out of my nose!'

The sailors trembled and backed away.

'That's not possible!' said Phlegm.

'It's not him. Finish the stitch, Finger, finish the stitch!' said Liver.

'Yes, yes, finish the stitch!' yelled several more.

But Finger knew his work. This was why the last stitch was tradition. Only the absolutely dead will lay quiet with a sailor's needle piercing their nose. Finger reached out and with a flourish similar to the one he had used to insert the needle, he withdrew it from the cloth and what was in between. Dawn was breaking, but nobody noticed, not even Tuesday, who was still crouched beside the wheelhouse looking on in utter terror.

In a panic, she attempted an owl call to hurry Vivienne back to her side, but it came out rather badly, and not very loudly.

'Who, whooooo,' she called.

She tried again, a little louder this time: 'Who, whooooo.'

The sailors spun about.

'It's the bird of death to be sure,' said Phlegm, his face white with fear.

'The owl is here, Cap'n. Lie down, lie down

and rest yourself,' said Gum, 'for an owl has come to guide you through the darkness to the afterlife.'

From within the shroud came another muffled scream: 'Aaargh! I'll not be going anywhere until every one of you is carved into little pieces and fed to the sharks by my very own hands. Now get me out of here.'

The men hesitated, and then one by one they nodded their assent. Daylight was creeping into the darkness like dye seeps into water.

'Don't you worry, Cap'n. We'll have you out in no time. You just hold still,' said Finger gently.

He admired his fine handiwork one last time, then took a knife and sliced open the shroud. His hands were shaking and indeed every man on deck was mute with fear as the shroud was pulled away and there before them, looking ghastly and broken, with blood oozing from the wound to his nose, lay Carsten Mothwood with the crow Baldwin still dead in the crook of his arm.

'Can he not die?' Vivienne whispered to herself, as she looked down from above.

She had stopped at the lowest yardarm, and from here she peeped over the furled sails and stared at the figure laid out below. The captain's head was fixed sidewards, and his arm was dangling unnaturally. One of his legs was still facing the wrong way but there was no disputing that Mothwood, at least for the moment, was alive. His face was a terrible mix of fury and pain. One eye scanned the shocked faces of the men about him while the other eye, clearly damaged by the fall, rolled around in its socket as if surveying the lightening sky. And then that eye swivelled to the yardarm and focused itself on Vivienne Small perched in the rigging.

'Vivienne Small!' gurgled Mothwood. 'There!'

The men stared at the captain in stunned silence. Surely he was hallucinating.

'There!' Mothwood shouted, spit flying from his mouth.

One arm attempted to wrench itself upwards without luck, broken as it was, and Mothwood was forced to lurch his head upon his shoulders, his eyes each going in opposite directions, his mouth leering furiously at his men.

'Above! The mast!' he bellowed, almost apoplectic with rage.

His men looked up and scattered, swords and knives at the ready as some made for the mast, some raced across decks and others took up positions port and starboard.

Though Vivienne made swiftly for the top of the mast, climbing with all the speed she could muster, she found that when she reached the crow's nest, she was trapped. Her right wing was too badly damaged for her to attempt a flying leap to one of the other masts. Without her wings, she would certainly fall to the deck far below, breaking as many bones as Mothwood himself.

From beside the wheelhouse, Tuesday watched Vivienne's plan unravelling. The pirates climbed higher, coming at her hand over hand. One of them grabbed at her legs and another hauled her backwards. Despite her best efforts, she was dragged swiftly down to the deck and tightly trussed. It was there that Vivienne Small, looking like a roast ready for cooking, faced the grim reality of a Mothwood newly awakened from death.

Finger and Gum helped the broken captain into a sitting position, so that he might see Vivienne helpless on the deck before him. As they did so, the body of Baldwin – tucked into the crook of the captain's arm – fell from the folds of the shroud onto the deck. At this sight, the captain howled.

'What has happened to my bird?'

'He died, Captain, from a broken heart. He laid himself beside you and died,' said Phlegm quietly, reaching down and picking up the stiff crow and placing him on the captain's lap.

Though he tried, Mothwood was unable to touch the bird. His fingers twitched a little at the ends of his useless hands and his face looked more wretched than ever.

'But not before finding the home of this savage,' Finger sneered, jabbing at Vivienne Small. 'And allowing us to fell the tree that has sheltered her all these years.'

'Baldwin,' said Mothwood, clearly distressed by the loss of his companion and not seeming to register Finger's words. 'Baldwin.'

Mothwood's speech was garbled and his movements erratic. Again his arm tried in vain to swing his hand to touch the bird, but the broken limb simply hung, apparently boneless and quivering. Gum lifted the bird away and set him against the mast, where the captain could see his shabby, black form. Then Mothwood's head raised itself crookedly and he looked about again.

One of the crew shouted out that they had spied *Vivacious* tied alongside, and an instant later Tuesday heard Baxterr snarling and barking down below. Then she heard him whining and yelping.

'No, not Baxterr,' she said silently to herself, clenching her fists until her nails almost pierced the skin of her palms. She longed to leap out and try to protect him, but what could she do in a fight against these large and vicious men? If she were captured also, then all hope would be lost.

She heard the winding of a winch, the creak of a rope running through a pulley. Tuesday's heart was beating so loudly as she pressed herself against the side of the wheelhouse that she was sure someone would hear it, but the men were otherwise engaged. When all had fallen quiet, Tuesday again peeped out across the deck. A terrible sight met her gaze. Bound on the deck was Vivienne, and beside her—bundled up in a fishing net—was Baxterr.

Chapter Sixteen

'Cut the creature loose,' Mothwood ordered.

It took two men to control the snapping, growling Baxterr as he was freed from the fishing net. The sailors secured a rope around Baxterr's neck, then pushed one of his paws through the noose and pulled tight to secure him. With a loop made out of a length of wire they muzzled him, twisting the ends until the wire cut into Baxterr's lip.

'No!' cried Vivienne Small. 'You'll hurt him!'

Tuesday, tears filling her eyes to see Baxterr treated this way, was nevertheless proud to see that Baxterr stood fiercely, snarling as best he could.

Mothwood attempted to get up from where he sat upon the edge of the table. He dismissed the help of Finger and Phlegm on either side of him. With great concentration, clicking his broken bones into some semblance of structure, he managed to stand upright. If you hadn't noticed that one of his feet and the knee above were both facing backwards, and that his head was on sidewards, you might have thought he was simply a man struggling with severe arthritis.

'Well, what do we have here?' he garbled quietly. 'Surely... it can't be ...?'

Gaining control of one arm, he swung his hand out towards Baxterr, who growled even more fiercely. Mothwood placed his hand on the top of Baxterr's head and stroked it.

Tuesday felt every pore in her skin shrivel to see Mothwood laying his hands on her dog. Baxterr's legs trembled. Mothwood's legs also trembled, but for quite a different reason. Then Mothwood leaned over Baxterr a little further and felt along his sides and drew out the damaged wing. Baxterr whined.

'So, Vivienne Small,' he said, his head clicking

202

towards his prisoner, who lay quietly in her bindings, 'a Winged Dog. Even if it is a puny little one. Where did you find him?'

Mothwood's voice was clearly meant to sound menacing, but instead it sounded as if he was talking under water. Vivienne did not reply.

'You know I've been searching for a Winged Dog for a very long time, Vivienne Small. It's so very kind of you to bring me one. Tell me his name.'

Vivienne said nothing though Mothwood lurched closer to her.

'His name,' he repeated.

'I shall never tell you!' said Vivienne defiantly. 'Not as long as I live!'

Mothwood gurgled, and Tuesday – in her hiding spot – realised he was attempting to laugh.

'Oh, I think you will, Vivienne Small,' Mothwood said. His voice was becoming clearer, as if he were getting used to the complexities of talking with a broken neck. 'But if I am wrong, and you do not tell me, then you will die. Actually,' he considered, 'with you dead, the dog will be orphaned and in need of a master. And a

Winged Dog cannot refuse a master, can it? Yes, much simpler. I think we might haul you up the mast and drop you to the deck, so you too can feel what it is like to have every limb in your body broken. Then I think you might have served your final purpose, Vivienne Small. Why, instead of this being my end, I do believe it's yours.'

Mothwood gurgled with laughter. Baxterr continued to growl and bristle with fury.

'You're wrong, Mothwood,' Vivienne said loudly and clearly. 'This isn't The End. I'm sure at The End, there'd be help. Help that you would never guess at. If I could get there, I'd go as fast as I could and be back, quick as a wink, bringing that help with me. But as *I* can't leave, I'll just wait for help to come. *As I am sure it will.*'

Tuesday, hearing this, was certain that Vivienne was telling her to flee, quickly, before Tuesday was discovered and was no use whatsoever to either Vivienne or Baxterr. But how? How could she possibly leave Baxterr here? Or Vivienne? Tuesday knew that if it were she, herself, captive on *The Silverfish*, then Baxterr and Vivienne would do anything in their power to rescue her.

But, unlike them, she was neither a fearless dog, nor a girl with a thousand adventures under her belt. She was just plain Tuesday, who had never had an adventure before in her life, and who knew nothing about rescuing anyone from the likes of Carsten Mothwood and his crew. It was her mother who had adventures. Her mother would know what to do. And Vivienne was right! Serendipity was almost certainly at The End.

Tuesday knew what she had to do. She snatched up the map cylinder from the deck and, with one parting glance to Baxterr and Vivienne, edged away from the wheelhouse and crept to the stern of *The Silverfish*. There was no time to lose.

Never had she felt so entirely uncertain. Part of her wanted to run back, throw her arms about Baxterr and be willing to die to save him from Mothwood's clutches. And the other part knew that if she did, and Mothwood killed her – and Vivienne too, no doubt – then Baxterr would be Mothwood's dog forever. She could not let that happen. She had to rescue him. She had to save Vivienne. She had got everyone into this trouble. She had to be the one to fix it.

The new day was announcing itself. Pink and red spears fanned up into the sky. For a single moment a golden sliver of light shot up from the horizon. Peering over the side of *The Silverfish*, Tuesday saw *Vivacious* was still there, bobbing on the sea, her sails furled. After capturing Baxterr, the pirates had left the little boat unguarded. A breeze sprang up, beckoning Tuesday to set sail.

Quickly she clambered over the railing of *The Silverfish* and down the ladder. She stowed the maps and unhitched *Vivacious* from *The Silverfish*. Ever so quietly, she hoisted the mainsail and unfurled the jib. In no time *Vivacious* was skipping away across the waves, as if the boat knew that this was a grand and urgent escape. All the while, Tuesday dreaded a cry from the pirates as they noticed *Vivacious* sailing off. Or, worse, Tuesday dreaded hearing the cry of Vivienne being dropped from the tallest mast onto the deck below. But no cry came.

Chapter Seventeen

'Hold on, Vivienne!' Tuesday muttered. 'I'll be back as fast as I can. Oh, Baxterr, I hope you can forgive me for leaving you like this. But I'll be back. I'll be back with help.

When she was some distance from *The Silverfish*, and there was no sign of the ship preparing to come after her, Tuesday swung *Vivacious* into the breeze and let the little boat drift on the brightening sea. She reached for the map cylinder and, pinning the tiller beneath her leg, she unscrewed the lid and drew out the roll of maps. As soon as she attempted to flatten them out, the breeze rippled their edges. The sails flapped and the boat rocked. The maps were large and detailed, and though Tuesday would have liked a table to lay them out upon, she had only her lap.

Behind her, the dark distant silhouette of *The Silverfish* was just a tiny speck on the vivid morning horizon. Tuesday scoured the maps, peering at the lines so carefully drawn and words so beautifully written. There was a map that documented carefully the Peppermint Forest and the River Rythwyck as it made its way to the Restless Sea. Another tracked the many paths through the Golden Valley and into the Mountains of Margolov. There were several maps for navigating the complex archipelago of the Islands of Xanchu and the peaceful Straits of Lillith, and there were maps that traced the roads that lead to the five Cities of Luminosity. But nowhere could Tuesday find The End.

Fear crept all over her skin. She was lost and alone. Without her dog. Without Vivienne. Adrift in a small boat on the open sea with no idea how to find her mother, and with maps that were seemingly useless. Tuesday looked up into the sky, trying to blink away the tears, and noticed that everything had changed.

While Tuesday had been poring over the maps, *Vivacious* had drifted into a mist as colourless as sadness. The cliffs, the horizon, all her landmarks had disappeared. And there was no breeze. Not even a whisper to fill the sails. Everything had become very, very quiet. It was as if she had drifted right off any kind of map into a strange, misty nowhere. When haste was all that mattered, she was standing still.

The sea was silken, molten silver-white. She trailed her hand through the water but, eerily, it gave no reflection. Tuesday jerked back her hand and tried to still her rising panic. The mist was close about her, sticking to her face, her hair, her clothes. It clung to the deck, too, and beaded on the woodwork. *Vivacious* was drifting aimlessly. It was so quiet that when Tuesday pushed the tiller across, hoping to find a way to fill the sails, the noise of it made her jump.

So began the longest day of Tuesday's life. A day where hope seemed impossible to hold onto. A day where she could only drift in an endless world of frustration and silence, trying all the while to still the terrible images that kept forming in her mind: Mothwood sitting up from the table, suddenly alive again in that awful broken body; Baxterr muzzled with wire; Vivienne being hauled up and up, then dropped from the tallest mast to the deck below.

Time and again Tuesday called out, hoping to be heard by someone on a nearby shore or perhaps another boat, but her voice only sounded small and strange. She tried talking to Baxterr in his absence, and then to her mother and father, but the conversations she was having were hardly helpful, so she gave it up. She counted in pairs to one hundred, practised her seven, eight and nine times tables, and thought through all the numbers with three in them counting back from one thousand. She unfurled Mothwood's maps and went over them again, trying desperately to spot any clue that might help her when this mist finally lifted. She searched into her backpack and found a slightly bruised apple and half a bottle of water. She ate the apple and sipped at the water, unsure how long it might have to last.

She thought longingly of watermelon, and once she thought of watermelon she thought of fresh pineapple and ripe mango. Then she thought of vanilla milkshakes and chicken pie, but that made her think of Baxterr, who loved pies of any sort.

'Stop it! Stop it,' she told herself. Her lips were stretched and dry, her mouth was furry with thirst. She sipped a little more from the bottle.

'Water, water, everywhere nor, any drop to drink,' she said, remembering it from a poem Denis had read to her. But now that she had thought of Baxterr again, her mind filled with images of him muzzled, snarling and afraid on the deck of *The Silverfish*. She wished she could summon up an entire army of warriors who would storm the ship and free Baxterr and Vivienne. She wished she could grow into a giant and crush Mothwood and his horrible crew with her own bare hands. She wished she could find Serendipity and hand the whole entire mess over to her, because it was too much for a girl, all alone, to manage. She wished she were at home, at the kitchen table, eating a huge plate of blueberry pancakes with Baxterr snoring at her feet. But wishing did nothing to change the fact that she was doing absolutely nothing. Her eyes burned with angry tears, but she rubbed them away with clenched fists.

'Tears are hardly going to help,' Tuesday told herself sternly. 'But what *is*?'

She tried to be logical. She needed help, but she didn't have Vivienne and she didn't have Baxterr. She didn't have a book either. Maybe there was another book, she thought, one that could help her, but somehow Tuesday doubted that anyone had ever written a book called *How to Rescue Your Friends from Pirates*, with step-by-step instructions and a useful diagram or two. She sighed, but decided it was worth searching the little cupboard at the front of the boat again.

She opened the hatch and felt all around, hoping for the greasy touch of oilcloth wrapping, but all she could feel were the waxy folds of a spare sail, and the rough weave of a coil of rope. At last, deep in the hatch, her hand came to rest on something else, something small and smooth and cool to the touch. She pulled it out and saw that it was a little metal container similar to a shoe-polish tin, though smaller. The container was hard to open, but once Tuesday had levered off the lid with her fingernails she found that it contained a cluster of rusty fishhooks, a book of matches, a silver whistle, a tiny fold-out pocket-knife — by far the smallest she had ever seen — and a small grey-lead pencil.

Tuesday looked at the fishhooks, but they were no use to her without a length of line. And anyway, she wasn't sure what she would do with a fish, even if she did manage to catch one. She wondered what the whistle might call up. Perhaps a genie who would grant her three wishes? She blew it with all the breath she could muster, but nothing happened except a loud, bossy whistling sound that disappeared into the thick silver mist. Tuesday lit a match and held it in her fingertips until the flame was almost touching her skin, then blew it out; she unfolded the blade of the pocket-knife, and although it was nice and sharp, she couldn't think of a single way that it might help her. Last of all, she took the pencil out of the tin. It was only small, but it had been sharpened to a decent point.

What was it that the Librarian had said? *It doesn't matter whether you write on a fancy laptop or an old typewriter, or, for that matter, with a pen on a paper napkin.* Or even, Tuesday thought, with a tiny pencil on ... She looked about. There was no paper of any kind except Mothwood's maps. She unrolled one and placed it upside down on her lap. In the far left corner at the top of the huge page, she began.

I know a girl who drifted on a colourless sea through a fog of nothingness, and this is the story of how she came to be there, she wrote. And then she wrote down everything that had happened since she sat at her mother's typewriter and set her fingers upon the keys. She wrote and she wrote, filling up the white space with words that were neat in some places, and messy in others. Sometimes the words went from left to right, but other times they went up and down, or diagonally, or in big curly spirals. Whenever her pencil was worn blunt, Tuesday would sharpen it again using the miniature pocketknife. She wrote until the back of the map was entirely covered, and the pencil was almost too small to grasp in her fingers. *And so,* she wrote in the last spare corner of space, *the girl had no way forwards, and no way back. No way down, and no way up.*

With that, she looked up and realised evening had come. A soft beam of light was illuminating her words. Not just illuminating them. The lines and loops and spirals of the words she had written were shimmering and trembling as if they were alive.

'Oh,' Tuesday breathed.

Her written words remained printed on the paper, but their silvery shadows were merging into one long, glowing thread that rose up and up above her, finding a pathway through the mist. Tuesday waited for the thread to wrap itself around her, to lift her up and take her … where? To find her mother? Back to Baxterr and Vivienne? Home? But the thread did not touch her. It only continued up and up, until the trailing end of it was hovering in front of her. Tuesday reached out and grasped the thread. It began to thicken. Now it was not so much a strand of silver thread as a length of shining woven rope. It continued to change before her eyes, splitting apart and stretching, becoming wider, developing rungs, transforming itself into a ladder. A silvery ladder that stretched far up into the mist. It was as if Tuesday were expected to climb. But to where? The ladder, glowing softly in the moonlight, ascended into nothingness.

Tuesday put a foot on one of the lower rungs. It felt quite safe. She gripped the ladder with both hands and still it held as strongly as if it were attached to a giant hook somewhere up above.

'There's no use being frightened now. You can save being frightened until later,' she told herself.

And with that, putting one foot above the other, and one hand above the other, she stepped off the deck of *Vivacious* and climbed. And climbed and climbed and climbed. Below, *Vivacious* became smaller and smaller.

'Don't go anywhere,' she called down to the boat.

After a while Tuesday's arms and legs began to shake with the effort. The mist closed in around her and she could no longer see *Vivacious* or the sea below. She rested for a moment, taking in a soft breath of wind that cooled her face. Above her the mist was thinning. Stars and a sliver of moon peeped from a far section of sky. She thought of her first flight from the window at Brown Street. Here she was, once more in darkness, holding on to something that might, or might not, bring her to safety.

She continued to climb for what seemed like a very long time. She could see nothing below. *Vivacious* was long lost from sight; only the ladder swung below her. And then, without any announcement, the mist was gone, as if Tuesday had finally climbed above it.

The ladder ended, and it wasn't attached to a giant hook. It was attached to *two* giant hooks in the middle of what looked like a square of ceiling. It appeared to be simply there, in the middle of the sky, as if such things were completely normal. In the middle of this square was a large metal ring.

'A trapdoor!' Tuesday said out loud. She clambered up, grasped the metal ring and pulled. When it didn't budge, she pushed. This time she felt the trapdoor give a little, so she pushed harder, and it opened smoothly without a creak or a groan. Tuesday slid her head and shoulders through the gap. There was hardly anything to see, just a tiny room with a very low ceiling and curtains for walls. It wasn't even tall enough for her to stand up in, although it was easily long enough for her to lie down. What *was* this place? A cupboard, perhaps? Why was there a cupboard in the sky?

Tuesday scrambled over the lip of the opening, crouching down so she didn't bang her head on the low ceiling. She closed the trapdoor behind her, shutting out the dark sky and the gently swaying rope ladder. There was no sound. She put a hand out to touch one of the curtained walls of the tiny room, and found that it moved easily. Edging forwards, she lifted the fabric. Beyond, in the dim light, she could see chairs and table legs.

'Could it really be?' Tuesday breathed in disbelief.

She crawled out and looked behind her. She had been beneath a buffet table with a white tablecloth. Beyond a stretch of tall windows was a balcony.

Tuesday had found her way back to the Library.

Chapter Eighteen

Despite Tuesday's relief at finding herself at the Library again, she dreaded running into the Librarian. She was sure that the Librarian would be very cross with her for disobeying orders and running off into the world of Vivienne Small. Probably, she would be angry enough to stop Tuesday from ever going back into that world. She might even send her straight home to Brown Street in disgrace, and Tuesday knew that she could not allow that to happen. Whatever came next, she would never, not ever, go home without Baxterr.

She ducked behind a chair and peeped over it.

She listened and looked, intently. Only when she was entirely certain she was alone in the room did she stand up.

The room looked different at night. For one thing, at the centre of each table was a beautiful egg-like lantern that gave out a soft, green light. On the buffet table were only two silver domes. Tuesday tiptoed softly across the room and by the greenish light read the words on the cards. The first said: I'm On A Roll And Couldn't Possibly Sleep. Under the dome was a tiny white cup full of a dark liquid that was certainly coffee. Tuesday wrinkled her nose, replaced the dome and moved on to the next one. The card read: Absolutely Nothing Is Going According To Plan, and under the dome she found exactly what she was looking for: a pot of chocolate custard topped with slices of fresh strawberries and a swirl of cream.

Without thinking, she took two of the little pots, one for herself and one for ...

'Oh, Baxterr,' she whispered, and as she put the second of the pots back under the silver dome, she felt tears gather. With all her heart, she wished that her dog were here, beside her, and not at the mercy of a vengeful pirate just back from the dead. She had to hurry. Tuesday had no idea what her wasted day adrift had cost Baxterr and Vivienne, but she felt that she must still bring help. If everything was not lost already, she reasoned, she had no time to lose.

Tuesday spooned the custard, cream and strawberries into her mouth. Even at high speed, the custard was seriously delicious and the taste of it was enough to make her feel a little less despondent. Somewhere in the Library, she would have to find the help that she needed, and quickly.

Placing the empty bowl back on the buffet, Tuesday crept towards the doors that led to the foyer. Though it was very late, she thought there might be somebody awake in the heart of the Library, in the great book-room itself. Her true hope, the one that she hardly dared admit to herself, was that the person she would find was the one person who could help her out of this terrible mess—her mother, Serendipity Smith, working at her favourite desk by the window.

Tuesday opened the door and edged out into

the foyer, keeping close to the walls, darting from pillar to pillar, once more shrouding herself in shadow. She made her way carefully, quietly, towards the doors on the far side and was almost there when she tripped on something rather large that had been left lying on the floor behind a pillar. Her head caught a sharp corner of stone as she went sprawling, her elbow hit the marble floor while her knee ploughed into something relatively soft.

'Oooooofffff,' came a voice.

As Tuesday collected herself she realised that the thing she had tripped over wasn't a thing but a person, and the soft object her knee had rammed into was that person's stomach. Further, the person she had tripped over, who was holding his middle and groaning, was Blake Luckhurst. *The* Blake Luckhurst.

'Blake!' Tuesday said in an excited whisper, trying to prevent herself from hugging him out of sheer relief.

She looked at him more closely, and her relief turned to concern. Even in the dim light she could see he had been badly hurt. There was clotted blood at his temple, one of his eyes was blackened and his jaw was swollen. He was covered in grime and dust, and smelled of dirty sports socks. Beside the patch of floor upon which he had been sleeping were seven or eight white pots, empty except for some remnants of chocolate custard.

'I'm guessing that absolutely nothing is going according to plan,' Tuesday said softly. 'What on earth has happened to you?'

'Unexpected mission failure,' Blake murmured. 'I think I've cracked some ribs.'

'What were you *doing* out there?'

'Oh, y'know, just trying to keep things interesting. A little nitric acid, a little sulphuric acid ... add some glycerine ... boom! I got carried away.'

Blake sat up and coughed, wincing as he did so. The blood at his temple was from a weeping wound on his head.

'What about you?' he said. 'Find that mother of yours?'

'No,' Tuesday said. 'You see, Mothwood has my dog – you remember – Baxterr? And he's going to kill Vivienne Small. I have to help them, but I can't do it alone. I went looking for help, but I lost a whole day just floating about in mist and then, well then I climbed up here. But now that I've found you, maybe you can help me. Although you don't look like you could be much help. But please, Blake, please will you help me? If you'd only seen Baxterr standing there, all tied up and snarling...'

'Whoa, whoa, Yesterday. That's not...that's Serendipity Smith's story: Mothwood? Vivienne Small? I thought you were writing some missing-mother thing.'

'Well, I...' Tuesday said, her brain whirring. She was perilously close to letting slip her family secret. 'The thing is,' she hurried on, 'I'm not making this up. I really have lost my mother, and I thought that if anyone could help me find her, it would be, you know, Vivienne Small.'

'But you actually got into a Serendipity Smith story?' said Blake incredulously. 'Man, that is crazy!'

'That's why I can't ask the Librarian for help,' said Tuesday. 'If she finds me here, she'll send me home. So you see, you're the only person who can help me – please say you will,' Tuesday begged, but Blake was completely distracted.

'I didn't even know it could be done,' he said. 'What happened when you got in?'

And so Tuesday told him how she'd fled down the stairs and walked to the Peppermint Forest and discovered Vivienne's tree house broken to rubble. She explained how she'd found *Vivacious* and learned to sail, and how Baxterr had nearly drowned and Vivienne Small had saved him. She told him about the raid on *The Silverfish* and how Mothwood had come back to life, and about the long and terrible sail through the endless fog.

'Hey,' said Blake, sitting up a little straighter when she finally fell silent. 'Not a bad effort, actually. I mean it's your first time so, you know, you can't expect perfection. I thought you were writing some soppy mother-daughter business. You know, haircuts and clothes and whatever girls are into. But your story – it's got violence, it's got drama, it's got tension. All you need to do is keep going. Get to The End.'

'But that's just it! Blake, I can't find The End anywhere. It's not on Mothwood's maps and Vivienne Small hasn't even heard of it.'

Tuesday was certain Blake was about to scoff at her, or tell her how stupid she was, or how great he was, or both. But he didn't. Instead, with a weariness that might have been caused by his hurt ribs and damaged face, or simply because he understood and even sympathised with her, he said quite gently, 'Yeah, The End, hey? The thing about The End is that it's not on any map. It's not a place, right? Well, it kind of is. I suppose you could say it's a place you have to reach, but it wouldn't have any actual coordinates. You couldn't program it into your GPS. The End is ... The End. It's where you get to when your story's done. There's no rushing it. It's more a feeling than anything else. That's what makes it so difficult.'

Tuesday sighed with exasperation and said, 'Why won't anyone listen to me when I say that I am not, repeat *not*, writing a story?'

Blake made a grimace of pain as he got slowly to his feet.

'You think?' He grinned. 'Well, let me show you something. Come on. The Librarian won't be about at this hour.'

Blake limped to a set of double doors at the side of the Library and pushed one open. It led to a smaller foyer with lamps fixed to the walls at regular intervals. Ahead was a single door.

'She'll never show you this room,' Blake said. 'She likes us to think it doesn't exist. But it does.'

A sign affixed to the door read: *No Admittance. Staff Only.*

'I figure as I'm keeping her in a job, I must be staff as well.' Blake smiled and held the door open for Tuesday to enter, before sidling in behind her. The door closed with a quiet shush. Inside the room was a smaller version of the great Library. Here the hanging lights were blue and there were rows of bookshelves filling the room. But this room felt entirely different. It was colder. There were no desks and no writers. Tuesday gazed at the shelves. There was something about the books. They looked as if they were made of glass. And when she looked closer some of them shimmered while others were entirely transparent. Some looked as if they were made of delicate wax and others from clear cellophane. Still others appeared to wobble as she passed. Inside them she could see slender pages. When she tried to read the spines of these strange books, the letters scrambled and disappeared, reappearing in different forms as if they were holograms.

'What's wrong with them?' Tuesday asked in a hushed voice.

'They're kind of... vulnerable.'

She reached out to take one from the shelf and her hand passed right through it.

'You can only touch your own story,' said Blake.

'What is this place?' Tuesday whispered.

'I'll show you,' said Blake, wheeling a ladder towards her. 'Let's find M.'

Together they walked between two long high shelves going deeper into the room. At last Blake found what he was looking for, although Tuesday was still confused. Looking at the books was as strange as opening your eyes underwater, or looking at trees through a rainy window.

'Here you go,' Blake said, shifting sideways on

the ladder so Tuesday could climb up beside him.
'Check this out.'

Blake pointed to one particular book on the
shelf right in front of them. Its cover might have
once been deep red, but the clear glass cover had
faded to a faint pink. There were words on the
spine where the name of the author ought to be,
but they were so vague that Tuesday could barely
read them.

'You have to look closely,' Blake said, climbing
down a rung or two to give her more space.

Tuesday narrowed her gaze until she could just
make out the ghostly silver letters on the book's
transparent spine. Tuesday McGillycuddy. *Tuesday
McGillycuddy?*

'That's my name,' Tuesday said. 'But it can't be
me. It has to be some *other* Tuesday McGillycuddy.'

Blake snorted.

'If it was mine why would it be so old and
faded?' asked Tuesday. 'Anyway, it's not a book.'

'That's right. It's not a book. *Yet.* And it's not
faded,' Blake said. 'It's so new it hasn't got its
colour yet. Nor its title. But open it up.'

'Can I?' Tuesday asked cautiously.

'Believe me, it's yours,' said Blake.

Tuesday reached out and very carefully touched the book. This time her fingers didn't slip through nothingness. They touched a cover that felt as fine and smooth as glass. She slid it from the shelf. It weighed almost nothing. Inside the pale transparent cover were delicate pages, tissue-thin and entirely blank.

'Look' she said, indicating the empty pages. 'There's no writing.'

Blake shrugged. 'It's just a beginning. It's taking form. That's what all these books are. Many of them never get finished. It makes the Librarian so mad when that happens. She hates this place. She'd prefer it didn't exist. But it has to exist. It's like the incubation room. All these ideas are trying to be books. But most of them won't make it. Hardly any in fact.'

'Look around you, Tuesday,' Blake said, in a perfect imitation of the Librarian that made Tuesday giggle. 'Look at my shelves! Everywhere I look, books begun and never finished!'

Blake went on in the Librarian's gravelly voice, 'Perfectly good books if only their writers would stay here long enough to get them done. I don't know what it is with writers these days. So many of them lack stickability. Yes, that's what I like in a writer, stickability. That young Blake Luckhurst, he's frightfully slapdash when it comes to punctuation, but he's got stickability – I'll say that for him.'

'So now,' Blake said to her as he clambered down to the ground, 'do you want to tell me you're not a writer? Managed to get here with a ball of thread. Got all the way into your story before you had your own version of what I like to call The Swamp of Doubt – when you don't know where you're going or what will happen next so you stumble about in a fog. And then you made your way back here. And lo and behold, there's a book with your name, no doubt the one and only Tuesday McGillycuddy in the whole world.'

I am a writer. Tuesday tried out the sentence in her head. *I am a writer.* It felt good. She looked again at the book in her hands. *My book,* Tuesday thought. And there was something on the cover, but it was shifting and changing. As she angled the book, she saw the word *Finding*, but when she moved it, the word changed to *Losing*.

Finding? Losing? Tuesday's heart raced. What did it mean? Was it Baxterr? Vivienne? Her mother? As she climbed back down the ladder, she saw Blake casually juggling his ball of silver thread. It curved in the air from one hand to the other. From the second last step of the ladder, Tuesday swiftly reached out and intercepted it mid-flight.

'Hey, give that back!' Blake snapped.

'Settle, petal,' Tuesday said, quickly returning it. She liked this helpful Blake and didn't want the arrogant, annoying Blake to return and spoil everything.

'You don't let anyone take your thread,' Blake said, holding it up to Tuesday. 'Not even for a minute.'

'But the Librarian took mine.'

'Yeah, I was dumb enough to let her take mine on my first book, too,' Blake said.

'But why does she do it?' Tuesday asked. 'If it's so important why does she take it off us?'

'So you don't go home before you're finished,'

Blake said. 'That way, the half-baked ideas in this room get to become real books and move next door, into the real Library. The Librarian's cool, but man is she obsessed with books.'

'I don't understand,' Tuesday said.

'The thread is how you get home, right?' Blake said.

'Oh, I see,' said Tuesday, feeling the light bulb blink on in her head.

'I mean, she's got a point,' Blake said. 'When you get home, it's easy to forget that this world even exists. You get on with all the other stuff and life goes by. Before you know it, you just lose the plot and your book never gets finished.'

'But how does it take me home?' Tuesday asked, gazing at Blake's thread and wishing desperately she hadn't let hers be taken by the Librarian.

'Easy. Just hold onto the end and throw it up in the air. It's pretty quick,' said Blake.

'So, if you wanted to, you could go home right now?' Tuesday asked him.

'Yep, right now,' he said, tossing the ball just a little way up, then catching it again. 'Just step outside and ffffft . . . you're gone.'

'And you could come back another day, and finish your story?'

'Sure. That's what we do. But I've got a deadline, y'know. And school and stuff. I haven't got time to muck around going backwards and forwards. Nice as it would be. I just don't have this book sorted enough. It's a bit of a mess ... as you can see.'

Blake's face looked very bruised in the pale blue light. The blood had congealed in his hair, but the cut above his eye was still weeping slowly.

'And my ribs are killing me,' he added.

'Give up?' Tuesday said with a grin. 'Not *the* Blake Luckhurst.'

For half a second, she saw a rueful smile on Blake's face, but then his expression changed. From the far side of the room came the sound of a door closing, followed by distinct footsteps. The lights flared to full strength, making the books on the shelves sparkle and shimmer, and Tuesday and Blake squint. The diminutive form of the Librarian appeared wearing a purple dressing gown and mauve high-heeled slippers with sparkly pom-poms on their toes. Her silver hair was encased in a fine net and her spectacular pearl earrings were conspicuously absent.

'Mr Luckhurst!' she announced in a low, irritated voice. 'Are you bleeding? Go to my private study, immediately! Heavens, what have you been blowing up *this* time?'

'Only a train, and an embassy. Oh, and a helicopter. Or two,' Blake said, guiltily. 'Sorry, Madame Librarian.'

'Off you go, right away. I'll be there momentarily to see to those cuts and bruises.'

Tuesday and Blake exchanged a quick glance before Blake sidled off. Tuesday took a deep breath, fearing that she was in for a far worse fate than the application of a bandaid or two.

'And Miss McGillycuddy,' the Librarian said, her voice as cold as an icicle. 'You've returned, I see.'

Chapter Nineteen

'Please don't send me home,' Tuesday begged. 'I know that I didn't do exactly as you said, but please, it's my dog. And Vivienne Small. They're out there in trouble and I have to help them.'

'Get control of yourself, child,' the Librarian said, her voice warming just a little. 'So, have you made progress? Tell me.'

And so, for the second time that night, Tuesday told her story.

'Good, good,' said the Librarian. 'I knew I was right about you. I think that this will be only the first of many stories from your pen, hmmm?'

'Well, that's all very well,' Tuesday said, 'but

I can't find my mother, which is why I came here in the first place. I can't find her and I can't find The End so I have no idea what to do next.'

'Well, let me ask you this, Tuesday,' said the Librarian, staring into Tuesday's blue-green eyes. 'Where did you leave your mother?'

'Leave her? I didn't leave her anywhere. I told you ... remember? That she went missing, and I came here to find her.'

'Then where did you last see her?' continued the Librarian.

'At home, of course,' said Tuesday. It seemed like a lifetime ago that Tuesday had set out for her last day at school before the holidays. As usual, she had crossed the road outside their house and, looking all the way up to the top storey, she had seen her mother in the window waving goodbye.

'Then it is plausible, is it not, that that is precisely where she is to be found?' the Librarian asked gently.

'I keep telling you. She was missing and I wrote about that on her typewriter and that's why I came here.'

'Exactly. You wrote about it and then you came

here. You came here ... but is it not within the realms of possibility, Tuesday McGillycuddy,' said the Librarian slowly and with a knowing look, 'that your mother – or should I say *Serendipity Smith* – has returned home while you, in fact, have been busy here?'

Tuesday gazed into the Librarian's animated face.

'You knew!' she said to the Librarian. 'You've known all along who my mother is. And you knew all along that she wasn't here.'

'Dear Tuesday, it's my business to know all that goes on in this place. But what kind of story would it have been, hmm? Girl arrived in a strange and wondrous world looking for her mother, and the first person she meets says: 'Oh, your mother, she's gone home.' And the girl goes home, and there's her mother. Tut, tut, Tuesday McGillycuddy. Where would the world be with stories like that?'

The Librarian turned on her slippered heels and began walking at a cracking pace beside the bookshelves. 'Come!' she called behind her.

'Wait!' said Tuesday. 'You let me go out there

into a dangerous world where Baxterr nearly drowned. Then we met Mothwood—who by all rights should be dead—and his vicious pirates. He's captured my dog and wants to kill Vivienne Small. He might have killed me for all I know, and all along you knew that my mother wasn't even here. They're still out there on Mothwood's ship with no help at all. Vivienne could be dead by now and...what kind of person are you?' she demanded, surprised at the rage she suddenly felt.

'Well, in my defence, Tuesday, Carsten Mothwood's resurrection was somewhat unexpected,' the Librarian said with a sheepish shrug. 'But in answer to your question, I can tell you that I, the Librarian of the one Great Library, am nothing more and nothing less than a lover of stories, of books, of the world of imagination. And I think you are, too. And tell me, honestly now, would you truly change a thing? Would you miss meeting Vivienne Small, or learning to sail, or discovering that dear Baxterr is in fact a legendary Winged Dog?'

The Librarian glanced at her with twinkling eyes as she led Tuesday through a door and across a sitting room. The Librarian swept back the long drapes and opened a set of French doors onto the balcony of the Library.

'What do I do now?' Tuesday asked.

'What you must do is find the ending for your story, before I change my mind,' said the Librarian. She almost shooed Tuesday out of the door.

'But I came here for *help*,' Tuesday said desperately.

The Librarian sighed.

'Come here, child,' she said, beckoning Tuesday to a white marble bench seat that overlooked a fountain and the gardens of the Library. They sat and the Librarian laid a tiny hand on Tuesday's knee.

'Do you know what serendipity is, Tuesday?'

Tuesday startled at the mention of her mother's name. But before she could speak the Librarian continued, 'A story is like a giant jigsaw puzzle: a jigsaw puzzle that would cover the whole floor of a room with its tiny pieces. But it's not the sort of puzzle that comes with a box. There is no lid with a picture on it so that you can see what the puzzle will look like when it's finished. *And* you have only some of the pieces. All you can do is keep looking and listening, sniffing about in all sorts of places until you find the next piece. And then you'll be amazed where that next piece will take you. Suddenly your puzzle can have a whole new person in it, or it can go from being on a train to a hot-air balloon, from city to country, from love to sadness to loneliness and back to love. Pieces can come to you at any time. When you're having a cup of tea or sitting on a bus or talking with a friend. It will be like a bell going off in your head. 'That's what comes next!' you'll think. And that's why it's serendipity. Serendipity is luck and chance and fate all tumbled into one.'

'But *how* do I end my story?' Tuesday asked. Her eyebrows scrunched together as she thought deeply about all the Librarian had said.

The Librarian smiled. 'I cannot answer that question. I am a reader. You are the writer, Tuesday. This is not your mother's world anymore. You've made it your own. So it is up to you to find an ending that makes your eyes sparkle and your heart race. That, dear girl, is the way to The End!'

Tuesday nodded.

'*Imagine*,' the Librarian whispered. 'Now off you go. Make me proud.'

'I will, I promise,' said Tuesday, getting to her feet. She was beginning, at last, to understand what she must do.

'And mind you take care of your thread,' the Librarian said. She smiled as she produced a much larger silvery ball of string from the pocket of her dressing gown. 'As you get more experienced, you'll get better at coming and going.'

'Oh!' said Tuesday, somehow very relieved to see it. It had a tiny cardboard tag attached to it, with the initials TM in very small letters.

'If you lose it, there's no way home,' said the Librarian.

'Oh, thank you!' Tuesday said, and impulsively she threw her arms around the Librarian.

'Yes, yes, very good dear,' said the Librarian, fending her off.

'If I wanted to, I could throw this up in the air right now and I'd be back in Brown Street?' Tuesday asked.

'You could,' agreed the Librarian.

Tuesday thought of a great many things at

once: of her mother's worried face, of her father's blueberry pancakes, of Mothwood reaching out to pat Baxterr, of Vivienne beside the fire telling Tuesday she'd come from an egg, of Baxterr towing her home from school on her rollershoes.

'But I won't,' Tuesday said, pushing the ball into her jacket pocket.

'I have a good feeling about you, Tuesday McGillycuddy. Now go!' said the Librarian briskly. 'There's no time to lose!'

Tuesday walked towards the doors back into the dining room, planning to return to *Vivacious* through the trapdoor in the floor.

'No, no, not that way. Use the stairs, much easier!' said the Librarian, pointing the way. 'Ladders! Of all things!'

Tuesday sprinted to the side of the Library and, using all the speed her legs possessed, she ran down the long flight of curving stone stairs. At the bottom, instead of the fields that had met her on her first morning, and the view across to the Peppermint Forest, there was a small jetty and a grassy shore. Waiting patiently, her sails already billowing in the new light, was *Vivacious*.

Chapter Twenty

Soon *Vivacious* was scooting across the Restless Sea. Yesterday's mist was nowhere to be seen. The sky was still dotted with stars, but they were fading. The moon had slipped far into the west. When Tuesday looked behind her, there was no sign of the steps she had climbed, nor the vast Library, only high green hills rising up from the sea. This time Tuesday was not troubled by the disappearance. She turned to the waters ahead and scanned for any sign of *The Silverfish*.

As she sailed, a dawn broke across the sky that was identical to the one she had seen the morning before. It began with the same pink and red spears, the same hushed beauty. And then a beam of golden light shot up into the sky and Tuesday was beset by the odd feeling that no time at all had passed since she had sailed away from *The Silverfish*. This was, of course, ridiculous because it had been sunrise when she had made her escape, and here again was the sun, rising again. In anyone's language, a whole day and night had passed. Nevertheless, Tuesday had a curious feeling of déjà vu.

And then the dark silhouette of *The Silverfish* loomed ahead of her. It was still at anchor! Tuesday's heart hammered in her chest. There was no way for her to hide her approach. Still, she sailed as stealthily as possible, bringing *Vivacious* alongside *The Silverfish* and securing the boat to the same metal ladder fixed to the side of the ship. No cries arose on deck. No one sounded any alarm. Tuesday climbed quickly, slipping over the railing. She darted again to the side of the wheelhouse and, creeping along its length, peered out over the deck.

Tuesday blinked. Was it possible? Everything was just as she had left it. There was Mothwood, hideously returned from the dead, and his men about him. Vivienne and Baxterr were both in the exact same position as before, as if Tuesday had simply blinked in her hiding place and not slipped away for a whole day.

Mothwood scratched Baxterr's ear with a malformed hand, his gaze fixed on the crumpled figure of Vivienne Small on the deck.

'Oh, do let's drop her,' he chuckled to his men. 'I would so love to see those little wings all bent and broken. Or will she tell me the dog's name?'

Vivienne, trussed in ropes and held tight by Phlegm, was silent.

'His name,' he repeated, his voice quiet and deadly.

Baxterr, hobbled and muzzled, sniffed the air and spotted Tuesday. Tuesday could see in his eyes that *he* didn't think no time at all had passed. Despite his undignified bindings, he wagged his tail, and indeed his whole body, with joy. Tuesday stepped boldly out onto the deck. For a moment Mothwood's men stared at her, and then they were upon her, grabbing her arms and marching her towards the tower of Carsten Mothwood.

'Ah, not another one,' he sighed, inspecting

Tuesday with his mismatched and malevolent eyes. 'And what species are you, midget or mouse?'

Tuesday said nothing, only gasped at the stench of his breath. It was a damp, rotting smell that seemed to contain scents of mouldering food, dead animals and the insides of drainpipes.

Baxterr barked.

Mothwood glanced at him, and registered the dog's delight at seeing Tuesday.

'So,' he said, 'the dog does not belong to Vivienne Small after all. He is *yours*.'

'He is my dog,' Tuesday said, with as much courage as she could muster. 'You will give him back to me, and release Vivienne Small.'

Ignoring her request, Mothwood lowered himself to her height. His voice grew gentle, consoling.

'He's a fine dog,' he said, a hideous version of a smile spreading across his face. 'What's his name?'

'No, Tuesday, don't tell!' Vivienne yelled. 'He'll...'

Phlegm's great hand was clapped roughly over Vivienne's mouth before she could finish.

'Shut her up! Make sure she cannot utter a word,' Mothwood ordered.

Phlegm took a handkerchief from his pocket, none too clean, and bound it about Vivienne's mouth, gagging her.

'Due south, lads, full sail, on the double,' instructed Mothwood, and every sailor save those holding Vivienne, Tuesday and Baxterr leapt to their stations.

'No,' said Tuesday. 'NO!'

Mothwood chuckled.

'Ah, so you don't want to go south? Then tell me the name of your dear dog.'

Above Tuesday's head, the mildewed sails of *The Silverfish* cracked as they unfurled. There was the screech and creak of rigging taking weight, and the yells of sailors at work. A great rattling noise at the bow indicated the anchor was being hauled up. Tuesday thought again of how Vivienne had brought Baxterr back to life after he almost drowned. *There are people who would kill to have a Winged Dog*, she had said then. *If the wrong person learned his name then you could lose him forever. It's part of a Winged Dog's magic. Their name is like a key, and you have to keep it safe.*

As if he could see all these thoughts as he

looked into Tuesday's face, Mothwood smiled and his smile was full of malice.

'Not going to tell? What a shame,' he said.

The Silverfish was leaving the Cliffs of Cartavia behind, and to Tuesday's dismay, the tiny *Vivacious* was cast adrift and left to bob alone on the sea. They were sailing south. South towards the dark dangerous waters Mothwood knew all too well. It would be impossible for Vivienne and Tuesday to return from there without *Vivacious* and even then it would take every stick of Vivienne's skills as a sailor. But *Vivacious* was lost. Why had she come back without help? What good could she possibly do here?

'The rat trap!' Mothwood demanded, and one of his crew swiftly brought out a wire cage, affixed to the top of which was a length of rough, fraying rope.

'Perfect accommodation for Miss Small, don't you think, *girl*? Well, come on, men, look lively! In she goes.'

Vivienne's face was unreadable as the men roughly crammed her into the cage, which was just big enough to contain her. When the cage door was bolted, Mothwood made a gesture to his men, who hurled the contraption over the side of the boat. Tuesday ran to the railing. Vivienne was suspended just above the waves.

'Let her go,' smiled Mothwood, and the men let the rope in the pulleys run. The cage plummeted into the depths below.

'Stop it! You'll drown her,' Tuesday screamed.

'Tell me the name of the dog,' said Mothwood.

'No!' Tuesday said.

'So, you want to be stubborn,' said Mothwood. 'How long will your friend last, do you think?'

Tuesday couldn't bear it. The cage was dragging through the water, completely submerged. Tuesday could imagine Vivienne holding her breath, pressed against the metal bars, crushed by the sea.

'Doggo,' said Tuesday desperately. 'Doggo!'

'Doggo?' Mothwood enquired.

He looked at Baxterr.

'Lift the cage,' he instructed his men.

The men hauled on the rope and the cage was hoisted out of the water to swing just above the level of the deck railing. Still crushed within the mesh, and also sodden, Vivienne glared at Mothwood with an expression of sheer fury. She sent a grim look to

Tuesday and almost imperceptibly shook her head. This was Vivienne Small, Tuesday thought. This was the fearless heroine who could get herself out of anything. And Vivienne was quite clearly telling Tuesday that she must not give in.

'Unbind the dog,' Mothwood said to Gum. Gum freed Baxterr's paw from the rope about his neck, and unwound the wire from his muzzle. Baxterr stood quivering, his senses alert.

'Hello, Doggo,' said Mothwood, leaning towards him.

Baxterr barked in a friendly way.

'Sit,' said Mothwood.

Baxterr sat and wagged his tail.

Tuesday gulped. What had she done?

'Stand,' said Mothwood.

Baxterr got to his feet again, tail still wagging.

'Very good,' Mothwood smiled.

'Bite her,' he said to Baxterr, indicating Tuesday.

Baxterr growled. He bared his teeth. He prepared to spring, but instead of launching himself at Tuesday, he launched himself at Mothwood, knocking him over and seizing Mothwood's leg between his teeth.

'Get him off,' Mothwood cried. 'Off!'

The men leapt to their captain's aid, trying to haul Baxterr off, but the dog would not let go. Blood dribbled down Mothwood's leg. Mothwood continued to scream.

'Let Vivienne go,' Tuesday said, in the most commanding voice she could muster.

The cage was dropped to the deck. The bolt was shot and a shivering Vivienne uncurled herself from its confines. Gum removed the gag from her mouth. Only then did Tuesday call Baxterr off. The men lifted their captain back onto his feet. After a few moments Mothwood recovered enough to speak.

'You will tell me the dog's name, his *true* name,' he said to Tuesday in a voice that was cold with wrath, 'if it is the last thing you do. And it almost certainly will be.'

Tuesday took a deep breath. She looked up at Mothwood and said:

'My dog's name is mysterry, with a double r,
and if he's your own dog, then he'll take you far.
He'll take you far beyond the most distant shores,
but no, Carsten Mothwood, he'll never be yours.'

Mothwood stared at Tuesday with a mixture of admiration and disdain.

'What have we here, then?' he said mockingly. 'A little poet? Be careful, *girl*, many have died by taking me on.'

Tuesday wondered, perhaps a little belatedly, if it had been a wise decision to break into verse. Mothwood liked to challenge his victims to a round of rhyming couplets and the price of losing was death. Never in any of the previous Vivienne Small books had any of his victims beaten Mothwood at this game. Not even Vivienne had ever battled Mothwood in this way. She had used every other skill in her armoury to deal with him rather than fight him with words. But Tuesday had begun. She took a breath and lifted her gaze to his cruel, pallid face above her.

'I'll take my chances,' she said boldly.

'Oh ho! Very well,' Mothwood said, his eyes sparkling, 'I challenge you to a duel in rhyming couplets. If I win, you will tell me the name of your dog and he will be mine. And your friend, Vivienne Small, will be my figurehead, lashed to the front of my ship until her bones rot into the sea. As for you, well, I'll keep the manner of your death a surprise until then. In the highly unlikely event that you win, then *The Silverfish* and her crew are yours. Do you agree?'

'I do,' said Tuesday, though her entire body was tingling with fear.

'We proceed until one of us fails,' said Mothwood. 'I'll toss.'

He drew a coin from his pocket. 'I choose heads.'

'No,' said Tuesday, who knew Mothwood's tricks only too well. 'Not that coin.'

She grabbed it from his hand and turned it over. Sure enough, it had a head on either side.

'Coin,' Tuesday called. Quick as a flash, Vivienne dug into her sodden pocket and flicked a coin to Tuesday. It was a gold coin with a mountain on one side and a lion's head on the other and Tuesday looked at it in wonder.

Carefully Mothwood inspected the coin and, seeing it was indeed a two-sided coin, he tossed it into the air, where it flipped over and over and over, as if in slow motion.

Chapter Twenty-one

'Lion,' called Tuesday.

Mothwood lurched to catch the coin, but it slipped through his fingers. Before the coin could hit the deck, Gum caught it and whacked it down on the back of one of his huge hands.

'Lion it is, Cap'n,' he growled. 'The girl starts.'

Gum reluctantly placed the coin back in Tuesday's palm. Then he ambled to the mast where, amid the many notches and scores from previous duels, he marked the timber with his knife, drawing a line across, and a line down. At the top of one column he carved the letter M, and at the top of the other column, the letter X.

All Mothwood's opponents were given the same letter, and so the mast was covered in many M's and many X's, but not once had the score in the X column exceeded the score in Mothwood's.

'Now chain them,' Mothwood said, and Phlegm grabbed Baxterr and Vivienne.

'No!' said Tuesday.

'I'll have no distractions,' Mothwood added coldly.

Tuesday watched helplessly as Vivienne and Baxterr were chained together beneath the scoreboard on the main mast.

'Well, get on with it, *girl*,' said Mothwood. 'They'll be free soon enough—if you win.'

'Then first, the rules,' said Tuesday, breathing deeply. 'A pair of couplets makes a turn. No half rhymes. Agreed?'

'Agreed,' said Mothwood.

'Right then,' said Tuesday. 'My first topic is ... family.'

Her gaze meeting Mothwood's, she said:

'My mother is Sarah, my father is Denis,
They often play bridge, but they seldom play tennis,

From Monday to Sunday they work and they play,
But what they love best is a girl called Tuesday.'

Tuesday's voice faltered at the thought of her parents, but the rhyme was good.

Mothwood's men gave a sentimental 'oooohhhh' at this, and Mothwood sent them a withering glare. With his knife, Gum made a mark in the x column. Mothwood turned his one good eye to Tuesday, while the other eye swivelled about as if following a passing seagull.

'Time,' he announced. And then he began.

'Through life you are gripped by time with her claws,
But at the moment of death, you'll find when it's
   yours,
That time has let go, that at last you are free,
But there's nowhere to go and nothing to see.'

Mothwood's men applauded, and Gum swiftly notched up a point for the captain. Tuesday suspected that Mothwood had known this pair of rhyming couplets a long time, and that he hadn't made it up on the spot at all. It seemed rather like cheating to Tuesday, but if that was his game, then two could play it. Tuesday took a breath, planning to hit Mothwood with one of her old favourites, but her mind drew a blank. Each and every one of her favourite couplets had suddenly abandoned her.

'Well?' Mothwood said. 'Cat got your tongue?'

He poked out his own tongue and breathed at her. The stench was so shocking that Tuesday said the first thing that came into her head: 'Food.'

Figs are delicious with soft cheese and ham,
Toast is quite scrumptious with butter and jam,
Eggs are improved by parsley and salt,
But milkshakes are best with strawberries and malt.'

'Aaaaaah,' said the pirates hungrily. A few of them whistled in approval. Gum put a second knife mark in Tuesday's column. Everyone's gaze turned again to Mothwood.

'Girls,' he said with a sneer.

'I know several sharks who have eaten small girls,
From the tips of their toes to the ends of their curls,

258

Did you know they scream loudest when their
eyeballs are chewed?
Especially, I'm told, when those eyeballs are blue.'

'Ha! Blue and chewed—they don't rhyme! That's a half-rhyme, at *best*,' said Tuesday triumphantly. 'You fail, Mothwood.'

Mothwood's face reddened, which was quite a spectacular sight on top of the deathly white sheen of his cheeks.

'It was good,' he screeched. 'It was good.'

He turned to his men. Gum deliberated with the men and then he said: 'We say it was good, Captain.'

And all the men roared out their agreement: 'It was good.'

It had become clear to Tuesday that the pirates would cheat and lie and do all that was necessary to ensure that their captain was victorious, but there was nothing she could do except take her next turn. She must not lose to Mothwood. She must beat him at all costs.

'Well, what paltry efforts will your puny mind come up with next, and please don't bore me with another simpering one about your *family*,' he said in a jeering tone.

The spectre of him was growing more ghastly by the minute. Mothwood loomed in front of her. Sweat had broken out on his forehead and both his eyes were weeping and bloodshot.

Tuesday's palms were sweating and she felt light-headed. She struggled to think of anything in reply. Vivienne gazed at her with a steady expression. Baxterr dropped his head onto his paws. Everything began to swirl in front of Tuesday. Vivienne, Baxterr, Phlegm, Gum, Stick, Liver, the sun blinding her eyes, the lift and fall of the ship as it sailed on. Then Tuesday focused on Mothwood.

'Mothwood,' she announced.

'Your head is on crooked, your body's decaying,
The legs you once walked on are twisted and swaying,
You can't feel the sunshine for cold bite of frost,
You may have fled death, but your life is still lost.'

Mothwood slumped against the mast and chortled.

'Really,' he said. 'I think I'm doing rather well.'

With this, he did a truly terrible thing. He swivelled his head all the way around until it was at last in its correct place. Both his eyes looked straight ahead. He smiled and took a small bow. This had an unsettling effect on everyone, especially Mothwood's men. They shifted uncertainly and would not look at one another. A chill crept over the deck. Mothwood spoke, breaking the spell for a moment, and his voice was quiet and menacing.

'Lost,' he announced.

> 'She will never again sleep gently at night,
> She will dread when she must extinguish the light,
> Every day, she will flinch at memories cruel,
> Of a dog she once loved and lost in a duel.'

This was a nasty trick. Fear crept along Tuesday's skin. A cold shudder of doubt ran through her whole body. She saw again that fragile beginning of a book by Tuesday McGillycuddy with the words on the cover changing from *Finding* to *Losing*. She couldn't do it. She looked at Baxterr and realised that Mothwood was right. She would lose him. She looked at Vivienne and imagined she was clearly expecting Tuesday to lose at any moment. Mothwood would lash Vivienne to the bowsprit of *The Silverfish* to become its figurehead. And Vivienne would die there. Baxterr would become Mothwood's dog. Tuesday would never escape. Mothwood would ensure that she died a grim and horrible death, the most horrible he could imagine.

At this last thought, Tuesday started out of her reverie. *Imagine. Imagine!* This was her only chance. If this didn't work, she was lost. *They were all lost.* She took a deep breath and closed her eyes. In a clear voice she said: 'Warning.'

> *'I should warn you my dog is about to take flight,*
> *He will break through your chains and before you*
> *can fight,*
> *He'll have rescued his friends, we'll be laughing*
> *and free,*
> *You'll never best Vivienne, my winged dog and me!'*

As she uttered the last words, Tuesday threw her arms in the air dramatically, as if casting a spell.

She heard something fall to the deck and, with a chill, watched as her ball of thread, dislodged from her pocket with the flourish of her arms, went rolling along the deck of *The Silverfish* towards Mothwood. Tuesday lunged after it. But Mothwood made one sweep with his long arm, and grasped the silver ball in his hand.

'Hmmmmm,' he said quietly. 'Precious, is it?'

Tuesday's shock ran across her face.

'Yes!' she said, before she could bite back the word and pretend the thread was of no worth at all.

Mothwood's eyes gleamed.

'Choices,' he said, teasing out a loose end of thread with his long fingers. And then, his voice filled with scornful pleasure, he began:

'You think you can win, but already it's done,
The game is all over. You've lost and I've won.
A choice must be made, not with heart but with head,
So what will it be now? Your dog or your thread?'

Mothwood held the ball out towards Tuesday.

'That's mine,' she said. 'That wasn't part of the game.'

'Not part of the game? Ohhh, Mothwood doesn't play fair,' he said in a whiny tone. His men snickered.

Tuesday shrugged.

'It's just a ball of string,' she said calmly. 'It's not important.'

She hoped Mothwood would believe her bluff. She knew there was no way she and Baxterr could get home without it.

'Oh, well then,' he said, 'if it doesn't matter I'll just toss it overboard.'

He lurched towards the railing.

'Are you sure it doesn't matter?' he asked, looking back at her.

'Yes,' said Tuesday, her jaw clenched.

And then she relaxed.

'Yes,' she said again, 'I'm quite sure it doesn't matter.'

And in that moment she suddenly and absolutely believed everything would be all right. If he threw the thread overboard, she might never get home. She might have to stay here in this strange land forever, but she would never abandon Baxterr and Vivienne. Not for anything in the world.

'Let's see if you truly mean that,' Mothwood said.

Mustering all his strength, Mothwood heaved the silver ball out over the ocean. It flew in a high arc, but instead of falling, it continued to rise. It soared upwards, high above the ship, twinkling and glittering. It was going much further and higher than Mothwood's ungainly throw could possibly have propelled it. Everyone on board was transfixed by this strange phenomenon. And then, as if the chains holding him and Vivienne were made of nothing more than papier-mâché, Baxterr broke free and took off after the ball of thread.

As she watched him go, Tuesday was reminded of Baxterr in City Park, leaping after a spinning frisbee thrown high in the air. But this time, Baxterr had no need to come down again. He spread his wings and flew up and up and up. Tuesday lost sight of the thread behind the looming shape of Baxterr. Though he was going further and further away from her, at the same time he seemed to be taking up more of the sky. This made no sense. Tuesday watched transfixed as Baxterr banked, and began to fly back towards the ship. But this wasn't her dog; this was an enormous dog. Truly Baxterr's wingspan was wide enough to match a glider's, his body was as big as a truck, his enormous legs were tucked up underneath him, and he had a smile from ear to ear. Baxterr glided over the ship, barking once. The boat quivered with the sound and the men ducked for cover.

'Now!' Vivienne yelled.

She grasped Tuesday's hand and pulled her towards the mast. The pirates, transfixed by the sight of Baxterr, were slow to react. Up and up the ladder Tuesday and Vivienne climbed. The men below did their best to pursue them, but the girls were faster. At the crow's nest they scrambled onto the narrow railing. Phlegm and Liver were gaining on them.

'Jump!' Vivienne yelled, grabbing fast to Tuesday's hand. And without being sure what was happening, only knowing she had to trust Vivienne, who always knew how to get herself out of any predicament, Tuesday jumped with Vivienne into nothingness. She saw the sea below her, the sun sparkling on the water, and then a great golden-brown dog appeared beneath them and *whoosh*, she landed in a soft warm pile of fur.

'Grab on!' Vivienne called.

Tuesday gripped the fur for all her might as Baxterr climbed up into the air and swooped away, holding Tuesday's ball of thread gently in his mouth. He circled once more over *The Silverfish*. Tuesday had a last glimpse of the pirates standing awestruck on the deck, and Mothwood screeching something incomprehensible, before Baxterr swept them away over the vast, rippling ocean.

Chapter Twenty-two

'Whoooo-hooooo,' whooped Tuesday and Vivienne as Baxterr made a spectacular nose-dive towards the sparkling water beneath them, and then pulled out of the dive at the very last moment to skim along just above the surface. Beside him, on either side, silvery flying fish leapt clear of the water, before dipping back beneath the waves.

Baxterr flapped his great furry wings and once again rose high into the sky.

'Doggo, you're amazing!' shouted Tuesday, who was holding tight to the shaggy fur at the back of Baxterr's neck.

'This is better than I ever imagined,' said Vivienne behind her.

Tuesday breathed the clear, crisp air and marvelled at the view spread out beneath them. From up here, the jagged white tips of the Mountains of Margolov seemed almost harmless, and the River of Rythwyk looked little more than a trickling stream.

'Look!' Tuesday called to Vivienne. 'See? By the Cliffs of Cartavia?'

'*Vivacious!*' cried Vivienne as she spotted her red boat drifting towards a beach.

'Baxterr? Can you take us down?' asked Tuesday, and Baxterr turned sharply and plunged seawards, making the girls scream with excitement and terror.

Changing the angle of his wings to slow his descent, he brought them in to land as effortlessly and gently as a bird lands on a tree branch.

Tuesday and Vivienne scrambled down from Baxterr's neck, and flopped onto the sand, exhausted and exhilarated. Baxterr dropped the ball of silvery thread from his mouth and nosed it towards Tuesday as if he wanted to play.

'I don't think we'll take any more chances with it!' Tuesday told him, picking up the ball and pocketing it, even though it was a little slimy from Baxterr's drool. 'Go fetch a stick instead!'

Baxterr, full of playful energy, cavorted up and down the beach, even though – in his overgrown state – it only took him four or five bounds to cover its length. Folding his wings up tidily, he flipped onto his back and rolled, making the sand squeak under his weight.

'You were very brave back there,' said Vivienne to Tuesday. 'Truly, you were wonderful.'

'Thank you,' said Tuesday. 'But it was only watching you being so brave, and the fact that I love Baxterr so very much, that gave me the courage.'

'What will you do now?' Vivienne asked.

'I will go home,' said Tuesday, with a grin. 'My dad is making blueberry pancakes for breakfast.'

'Then I shall miss you, Tuesday McGillycuddy.'

'Perhaps you could come … home with me. It can be done. I mean, Mum bought Baxterr home,' Tuesday said. 'And I know my mother and father would be very pleased to have you.'

'Oh no, if it's all the same to you, I have a new tree to find and a house to build. And besides, I don't think I'd be very good at maths and all those other things you do at school.'

The two girls stood there for a moment in silence.

Then Vivienne smiled.

'Goodbye, Tuesday. You are the bravest person I have ever met.'

'Goodbye, Vivienne. It was the most wonderful thing to have an adventure with you. Thank you for everything.'

Then Tuesday watched with admiration as Vivienne sprinted towards the water and—just as she was about to get her feet wet—leapt up and spread her leathery blue wings, propelling herself over the water and onto the deck of *Vivacious*.

'I'll never forget you!' called Tuesday, as her friend set the sails of *Vivacious* and steered the vessel out of the cove.

'Ruff!' called Baxterr, who was up on his feet, towering over Tuesday.

From the helm of her boat, Vivienne gave Tuesday and Baxterr a salute, before a gust of wind filled the sails of *Vivacious* and set her skipping away over the waves.

'Well, doggo,' said Tuesday, ruffling her hand through the fur of Baxterr's leg. 'Shall we do it? Shall we go home?'

'Hurrrrrr,' said Baxterr.

Tuesday surveyed him where he stood, joyfully huffing above her.

In a gentle voice, she said, 'I promise we'll come back and you can grow big again and you can fly and fly and fly. But for now, we have to go home, and you need to get back in through the window and live in the house and sleep in your basket in my room.'

'Ruff,' agreed Baxterr.

'So, I guess you know how to do that?' Tuesday asked.

'Ruff,' said Baxterr.

Tuesday closed her eyes and when she opened them again, Baxterr was a smallish dog, with a whiskery face and shaggy hair in every conceivable shade of brown and he was doing what he always did: grinning up at her.

'Isn't it funny,' Tuesday said, lifting him up

and holding him tight to her chest, 'to think that inside every small dog there might be a great big dog with shaggy wings, just waiting for a chance to fly.'

Tuesday reached into her pocket and brought out her thread. She found the end and wrapped it around her hand. Then, with the biggest heave she could muster, Tuesday threw the ball of string into the air. The silver ball went higher and higher, just as it had done on *The Silverfish*. But this time Tuesday and Baxterr were going with it, whizzing up and up and on and on through a morning sky. Tuesday glanced back, but already the sea and *Vivacious* and Vivienne Small had melted away into the whiteness of the surrounding clouds.

Chapter Twenty-three

In the writing room on the top floor of the tallest house in Brown Street, Denis McGillycuddy and Serendipity Smith were much too absorbed in their worrying to notice a strand of silver thread sneak in through the open window behind them and start coiling itself into a ball. It was not until they heard a resounding crash that they both spun around to see Tuesday flailing on the floor and Baxterr leaping from her arms, tail wagging.

'Tuesday!' they both yelled, their faces alive with relief and surprise. 'Baxterr!'

Tuesday sat up and grinned.

'I'll get better at the landings,' she had time to say before her parents were upon her, crushing her in enormous hugs.

'You did it!' said Serendipity.

'You made it!' said Denis.

'We made it,' said Tuesday, pulling Baxterr into the fold of their embrace.

'I'm so pleased to have you home,' said Serendipity as they slowly untangled themselves from each other. 'And look at that thread!'

'Mum, Dad, it was amazing,' Tuesday said, and without getting up from the floor, her parents sat and listened as she told them all that had happened to her. Serendipity rolled her eyes as Tuesday described Blake Luckhurst, and smiled when Tuesday told her about the book in the great Library that had the name Tuesday McGillycuddy on its spine. Denis shuddered with fear when Tuesday described how Baxterr had nearly drowned and sighed with relief at the part when Vivienne revived him. Serendipity shook her head sorrowfully in the part where Mothwood came back to life, and clutched Tuesday's hands when she told of Baxterr being captured and hobbled on the deck. Denis chuckled with pride when Tuesday explained how she had bested Mothwood in a game of rhyming couplets. He had her repeat the one about food four times, and said that it was the best of the lot, and that truly, she had deserved to win. Baxterr barked excitedly when Tuesday described how he had taken to the skies to catch the thread and then caught the girls on his back as they jumped from the crow's nest.

And when the story came to an end, Denis jumped to his feet. 'You must be starving,' he said.

'I am hungry,' said Tuesday. 'Very hungry. What time is it? I feel as if a week has gone by.'

'Well,' said Denis, consulting his watch, 'technically, it's lunchtime, but as the night has been long and your victory hard won—and a story all done—I think blueberry pancakes are in order. C'mon, Baxterr, let's see what we can find for you too, doggo.'

As Denis galloped downstairs with Baxterr trotting hungrily at his heels, Tuesday and Serendipity looked at one another. Serendipity sat down on the chair at her desk and took her daughter in her arms.

'You've done something wonderful,' her mother said. 'Now all that remains is for you to write it down. Was Mothwood terrifying?' she asked, as she stroked Tuesday's hair.

'He was terrifying,' Tuesday said. 'Especially since he was only half alive.'

'I'm afraid that was my fault,' said Serendipity. 'I was trying to get to you, in whatever way I could. I wrote him back to life, because I thought that if I kept *Vivienne Small and the Final Battle* going somehow, then I'd be able to return to the world of the story and bring you home. I shouldn't have tried to interfere in your story—it was a terrible mistake.'

'Well, I suppose I made a mistake when I went looking for you in the first place. I thought you were stuck. But I guess you were here for almost all the time I was there!'

'I'm sorry I was so late home, but I so wanted to finish my book. I felt absolutely compelled to push on to The End,' Serendipity said.

'Baxter and I made a wish at the fountain on the way home from school,' said Tuesday.

'Ah,' said Serendipity. 'Wishes are very powerful things.'

'But if you hadn't stayed late, then I'd never have gone at all,' said Tuesday, smiling.

'And when coincidences happen at precisely

the right time,' said her mother, 'that is what you call ...'

'Serendipity!' called Denis from downstairs. 'Tuesday! Breakfast in ten minutes!'

Serendipity and Tuesday looked at each other, and laughed.

And then a thought occurred to Tuesday, and her face grew grave.

'Mum, did you know that the Librarian knows our secret? She knows that you're my mother. I didn't tell her, she already knew. But I did tell someone. I told Vivienne. I had to. I was so desperate to find you.'

'It's all right, darling. I hardly think the Librarian, or Vivienne, are going to have it splashed on the front page of the newspaper, do you?'

'Mum, there's one other thing that's puzzling me,' Tuesday said. 'About Vivienne.'

'Yes?'

'When I talked about you with Vivienne she seemed to think you were an imaginary friend.'

'Hmmm, that's a good way of putting it. Do you know what I think?' mused Serendipity, looking out the window that was still open to the day. 'I think that characters in stories have their own lives to live, and we are not important in those lives. When we are with them, we are as real to them as they are to us, and they allow us to share in their adventures. But when we leave, we slowly fade away from their minds. Not entirely, of course. To them, we become something like a dream, or a distant memory. I think that while it is our business to keep them vivid in our hearts and minds, it is not their business to do the same for us.'

'But if *you* fade away into Vivienne's dreams, will I, too?'

'I expect so, my love.'

'Oh,' said Tuesday, feeling a little crestfallen.

'Don't be sad, darling. You can meet her all over again, whenever you want to. That's the wonderful thing about it.'

'And what about Mothwood? You meant for him to die at the end of your book, but then you changed it.'

'I did, and those terrible changes I made are right there in the bin.'

'But we both know that more happened after that!' Tuesday protested.

'Yes, my love, but that's part of *your* story, not mine. So, let's deal with the ending of *Vivienne Small and the Final Battle* story, properly and finally, shall we?' said Serendipity.

She drew the manuscript towards her and picked up the last page. This she threaded into the typewriter. Tuesday read aloud the final lines Serendipity had written there.

'*Vivienne lay down in her hammock to sleep, although her right ear, the one with the pointed tip, remained as tuned as ever to the call of adventure*,' it concluded.

'It's perfect,' Tuesday said.

'Thank you.'

Serendipity flipped open the little silver box that sat beside her typewriter and delicately plucked out the short thread of words that lay within.

'You love writing, don't you?' asked Tuesday.

'I do,' said Serendipity.

'It felt so real, but did all of those things truly happen to me?' asked Tuesday.

'When it's done well,' said Serendipity, 'it can feel as real as sunshine on your face. It can taste like mint on your tongue. It can sound like lightning, or the scream of someone you love dearly. It wouldn't be a good story if we, the writers, didn't totally believe in it, would it now?'

'Do you think it will ever happen to me again?' Tuesday asked, as the smell of pancakes wafted up four flights of stairs.

'Well,' and here Serendipity touched Tuesday's ball of thread on the desk, 'I don't think there's any doubt of that. You can start writing it all up over the holidays if you want to.' Serendipity smiled at Tuesday. 'But right now is not the time for a beginning. For now, it's ...'

Tuesday nodded as she looked at the page sitting in the typewriter.

'Here. Why don't you do it?' asked Serendipity.

'Really?' said Tuesday. She rolled the paper down a line or two so there was a blank space below the final sentence her mother had written. Lifting the two small words off her mother's hand she slipped them onto the page. The letters didn't turn to silver thread and loop around her hands. They sat there nice and black and steady on the page.

THE END

ACKNOWLEDGEMENTS

WE WOULD LIKE TO ACKNOWLEDGE all our children for the myriad ways they inspire and amuse us. For this book we must especially thank Isabelle and Xanthe, who modelled for Tuesday and Vivienne, listened to various drafts and made brilliant suggestions when we were stuck. And Byron who offered wonderful insights into the nature of adventure. We thank the readers (of all ages) who told us what they thought along the way: Lily McCann, Milton Kapelus, Isobel Andrewartha, Hannah Warwarek and Jessica Hancock. We would also like to express our gratitude to the many members of our extended families for love, support, food, humour and encouragement. And to John and Rowan, for being there at our own versions of Brown Street, when we come in to land at the end of a long day.